THE SKULL CRUSHER

SKULL #2

PENELOPE SKY

Hartwick Publishing

The Skull Crusher

CONTENTS

1

CASSINI

The blacked-out Hummer approached a three-story building in the heart of Florence. Just a few blocks from the biggest church in the city, there were no lights in the windows and it seemed deserted.

I hadn't said a word.

Neither had he.

A garage door opened on the side of the building, and one by one, the vehicles descended into an underground garage. Armed men were already there as the vehicles were parked.

I sat in my black cocktail dress, my left ring finger comfortable now that my wedding ring had been ditched. I'd tossed it on the table like it was garbage—because it was garbage to me. My hand throbbed slightly from the way I'd struck Lucian. I could have broken my hand, and I still wouldn't have regretted it. Hopefully, his cheek was red for a week.

Balto stepped out of the car and greeted his men.

I stepped out and suddenly felt like I was on display in

my backless dress and heels. All the men turned their gazes on me, lust and aggression in their eyes. They looked me up and down like I was a model on the runway. Their guns were lowered, but their eyes were packed with violence.

Balto gave orders to his men, and they immediately dispersed. The underground garage was full of armored vehicles and shelves of guns and ammunition. It was a battle station where men prepared for war.

I crossed my arms over my chest and lingered in the back, unsure what was next. Would we stay here? Or would we return to his place?

Balto came back to me when he was finished. "Let's go."

"Where, exactly?"

He didn't answer me as he walked off. On the other side of the garage was a brown pickup. It wasn't shiny or new, instead, at least a decade old and unremarkable. It didn't seem like the kind of car a crime lord would drive. Lucian had a Ferrari, and he'd picked out a Bugatti for me. Balto didn't seem to care what he drove.

I followed behind him, not out of obedience, but because I didn't want to hang around fifty armed men who didn't know how to keep their eyes to themselves.

We both got into the truck, and Balto drove to a gated opening on the backside of the building. He emerged onto the street then drove away, his eyes scanning the roads and sidewalks along the route.

I eyed the old radio in the center console. It still had a CD player, something that was obsolete in modern times. He didn't have a backup camera or a digital speedometer. The truck had to be at least a decade old, and for someone who owned an entire building for himself, that didn't quite make sense.

I looked at him from my side of the truck, seeing the muscles of his jawline shift and move slightly as he remained absorbed in his thoughts. He was a pretty man—but a man clearly violent and unpredictable.

"Yes?" he asked, his voice filled with annoyance.

"I can't look at you?"

"You aren't looking. You are staring."

"You stare at me all the time."

"That's different." He drove with one hand on the wheel, the other resting against the windowsill. "I own you. I can stare at my property all I want."

"You don't *own* me." Lucian had said those words to me for the last two years, and I was sick of being someone's property. I'd been sleeping with Balto because he pleased me, but I didn't sign my soul over to him. "You said you would kill him for me if I asked. You said you would help me if I asked."

He turned his gaze on me, ignoring the road ahead. Lights from the street and passing cars reflected in his eyes, adding to his terrifying image. "And you didn't ask. I gave you a way out, and you refused to take it. I took you because I wanted you, because I wanted to punish my enemy and please myself at the same time. Make no mistake, baby. I did this for me—not you." He turned his gaze back to the road and arrived at the compound surrounding his building. He pulled inside, where his men were guarding the property.

"You can't be serious." Did I just leave the imprisonment of one dictator only to be a prisoner of another?

"Dead serious." He killed the engine and hopped out of the truck.

I followed him, feeling his men stare at me as my heels tapped against the asphalt of his parking lot. "After everything that man has put me through, you're just going to do the same thing?"

He entered the building then punched in the code for the elevator. "I'm sorry if I gave you the impression I was a good man."

"You did offer to help me."

"And you didn't take that offer." The doors opened, and he stepped inside. "When I realized you were Lucian's wife, I found another way to torture him. I killed his brother right before his eyes, and now I'll fuck his wife every night. I will torture him until he submits to me—and I will enjoy every second of it." He hit the button, and the elevator rose to the top floor. He stepped off and pulled out his wallet and keys before setting them on the table.

"And you just expect me to be okay with this?"

"Yes." He pulled off his shirt and tossed it on the couch.

Normally, the sight of his perfectly chiseled physique would send me to my knees, but my rage made me immune. "Well, I'm not okay with it. If you expect me to be your willing prisoner so you can play these games—"

"They aren't games. This is war."

"Whatever. I'm not going to—"

"You will do exactly as you're told." He didn't raise his voice, but when he flexed all of his muscles and commanded all the power in the room, he suddenly seemed bigger, louder, and bolder. "In case you haven't noticed, I'm not a kind man. I'm heartless. I'm cruel." He slowly stepped toward me, his blue eyes dark with hostility. "I own this city—and I own you. Fight me all you want. I get off on that sort of thing. But you'll just make it harder on yourself."

Sleeping with him must have clouded my perception. I was too busy coming around his dick to truly understand the kind of man I was dealing with. At the opera house, he'd killed two armed men with his bare hands and practically made Lucian shit his pants. Obviously, he was dangerous. He'd earned his reputation for a reason. I was stupid to think he would be any different with me. "I'm a fighter. Always have been. Always will be." I placed my hands on my hips as I stared him down, refusing to show fear even if it was the smart thing to do.

A soft smile emerged on his lips, but his eyes were still lethal. "That works for me."

HE HAD EXTRA BEDROOMS, so I picked one that had a private bathroom and called it home. It had a large TV and a nice view of the city landscape. There were empty dressers and a closet filled with nothing but hangers.

I didn't have any clothes.

All I had was this backless dress and the black thong underneath.

But it seemed like Balto only wanted me naked, so it didn't matter.

I sat on the bed and thought about my situation. I woke up that morning as Lucian's wife, a miserable prisoner. My life had no meaning because I was nothing but a puppet. I obeyed because my honor bound me to do so. But now that I was Balto's prisoner, I felt no such obligation. I didn't owe him anything, so I had no interest in being cooperative.

I didn't know what I should tell my brothers. They would probably be pissed, but they might also be relieved. They hated Lucian so much that they might prefer Balto. But then again, Balto was a criminal of the underworld, so maybe I was in a worse situation.

I waited for Balto to come to my bedroom and demand sex from me, but he never did.

I wondered if there was a chance I could escape. If I ran away from Balto and succeeded, I wouldn't be breaking any promises. I could actually be free. I had no idea where I would run, but Case and Dirk would be able to help me.

Maybe Balto kidnapping me was the best thing that had ever happened.

I fell asleep waiting for him and woke up the next morning with my hair a mess and my makeup smeared across the pillow. Instead of looking like a prostitute who woke up with a hangover, I chose to wash my face and go with a natural look.

I heard the TV in the other room, so I left the bedroom and found Balto sitting at the dining table. A mug of coffee was in front of him as he watched the news on the TV. He must have heard my approach, but he didn't bother looking at me.

I eyed his breakfast—egg whites and tomatoes.

"I need something to wear."

He brought the mug to his lips and took a drink. "You are wearing something."

"I can't wear this forever. And I need new underwear."

"I bet." He set the mug back down. "Your panties are usually soaked."

I narrowed my eyes at the comment.

He finally looked at me, the smile in his eyes. "You know it's true."

"Trust me, they are dry right now."

"Take them off and prove it to me." He sat in the hardwood chair shirtless, his thick arms on display with muscularity. The veins ran all the way down his forearms to the tops of his hands. For a man who broke the law for a living, he didn't bear any scars. He was flawless everywhere.

"I'd rather not. Can I borrow your truck to do some shopping?"

"And some money?"

"No. I have money." My bank account had been piling up with cash over the last few years. My stake in the pasta company gave me profits I didn't deserve. I'd tried to convince Case and Dirk to drop me since I didn't contribute to the business at all, but they'd refused.

He relaxed against the back of the chair and stared at me, his mood souring once more. "Where did you get this money?"

I crossed my arms over my chest. "None of your business. That's where."

His eyes narrowed. "Answer the question."

"What does it matter? It's not like I'm asking you for money."

"It matters." His voice lowered. "I don't want you using that asshole's money. You use my money."

"I didn't have a chance to grab anything before I left, so

no, I'm not using his money." I wouldn't use Lucian's money even if I had it. I'd rather throw it in the river.

"Then where did you get this money?"

"From working," I said like a smartass.

"And where have you worked?"

"You know, I don't appreciate being interrogated."

"And I don't appreciate asking the same question twice. If you were a man, you would be dead right now. So answer the question before I really get angry." Half of his plate was still full, but he didn't take another bite. His fingers rested around the coffee mug as he stared me down.

"My family owns a business. My cut gets deposited into my account every month."

"Your family knows about Lucian, but they never tried to save you?" he asked, his eyebrow raised.

"It was my decision to accept Lucian's offer. They've never been happy about it, but they've let it go."

He shook his head slightly.

"And I wouldn't want my brothers to risk their necks for me. It's not their problem."

"That's not true. When it comes to family, one person's problem is everyone's problem."

I continued to stand there with my arms across my chest, annoyed that I found this man sexy in the morning light. His shirtless body was ripped with the kind of muscles Lucian couldn't even dream of. Balto was on the leaner side, but since he was predominantly muscle, he weighed as much as an ox. "Anyway, can I borrow a car to pick up a few things?"

The corner of his mouth rose in a smile.

"What?"

"How stupid do you think I am?"

I should have known it wouldn't be that easy.

"You can wear my boxers and t-shirts for now."

"And if I want to leave the house?"

"I'll have one of my men pick you up a few things. Just write down your sizes."

"What if I want to pick out my own things?"

He stared at me coldly, as if he didn't hear what I said.

"Hello?"

He didn't blink. "I'll pick out your things. I have great taste."

"So...all you're going to buy me is lingerie?"

His eyes turned slightly playful. "Most of it, yes."

"Well, I'm not going to wear it."

"So, you prefer to be naked all the time?"

"No, I—"

"Then you'll wear what I buy you." He rose to his feet and grabbed his plate. "You want some breakfast?"

"Depends. Do I have to eat that?" I glanced at the remaining egg whites and tomatoes on his plate.

"Eat whatever you want." He carried the plate into the kitchen.

I followed behind him and helped myself to a cup of coffee. When I opened the fridge, I was disappointed to see nothing but chicken, fish, and vegetables. There was no pancake batter, bacon, or stuff to make a sandwich. Was this really a man's fridge? "Please tell me the fridge doesn't always look like this."

He washed the plate then placed it in the dishwasher. "Yes."

I shut the door because I'd rather not eat than eat egg whites. "Not even a box of cereal?"

"I haven't had cereal since I was eight."

It didn't surprise me that he had that perfect body, but he made such a sacrifice to maintain it. I couldn't give up burritos and cheese if my life depended on it. Maybe it would cut down my lifespan, but I didn't care. I'd rather die young and happy than old and skinny. "Then I'm gonna need the car to go to the store—because this isn't going to work."

"Make a list. I'll pick up whatever you want next time I'm out."

"You don't have someone to do that for you?" He had fifty men outside. Not one of them could pick up some groceries?

"I don't let anyone into my building."

He was more paranoid than Lucian. Lucian had staff all over the property, from maids to gardeners. I carried my coffee to the dining table and sat down, still wearing my black dress that cost Lucian thousands of euros.

Balto came back into the dining room and stared down at me. Like a statue looming over its admirers, he intimidated me with his height and size. "Take off that dress."

"I will when you get me some clothes."

His hand moved to the table next to mine, a silent threat. "I don't want anything that man bought you in my house. Change your clothes and throw away that dress. Do it now, or I'll do it myself."

Lucian spent most of his time ignoring me, and when he wasn't ignoring me, he didn't boss me around quite this much. Balto was a million times more threatening, getting under my skin without actually touching me. I wasn't sure if he would actually hit me the way Lucian had, but I didn't want to take the gamble. I rose to my feet and left the steaming mug of coffee behind. The only defiance I could offer was not looking at him as I headed down the hallway to where his bedroom was located.

The bed I'd lain in dozens of times was there, the sheets kicked away and messy. I opened the drawer of his dresser and fished out a pair of boxers and a t-shirt that were many sizes too big. I dropped the dress and put on his clothes.

His cotton shirt was so soft, and it smelled like it'd just been washed. His boxers were too big, so I had to roll them several times to keep them from sliding down my waist. I walked back into the dining room and found him exactly where I'd left him. "Here." I threw the dress at him, along with my black thong.

He tossed the dress over his shoulder then stretched the black thong between his hands. With his eyes downcast, he pulled on the lace then looked into the lining of my underwear. He must have seen something he liked, because he gave me that boyish grin, the one where one corner of his mouth rose. "That's my baby..."

2

BALTO

When I'd met with Lucian, I'd anticipated his decision. The man was so arrogant, it made him stupid. Or maybe he just was stupid. I wasn't entirely sure. But either way, I knew he wouldn't cooperate with me.

And that was fine with me—because I got her.

Lucian didn't stop me because there was nothing he could do. He provoked me into becoming his worst nightmare. He turned me into this vengeful beast. Truth be told, I didn't even care that much about the skull diamond. And I could still destroy my enemies without his bombs.

Cassini was more valuable than both.

Especially since she actually meant something to him. Every night, he would go to bed knowing I was plowing her like a whore. I was dumping my seed inside her and replacing all the evidence that he had been there at all.

It would eat him alive.

It was a better punishment than death.

I knew he would have preferred me to kill Cassini rather than rape her.

But she was much more useful alive than dead… because she was sexy as hell.

I hadn't taken her to bed yet because I knew she was livid with me. She liked me as her secret lover, but she didn't like me as her owner. She confided in me how she got stuck in that position in the first place, so I should pity her, not take advantage of her situation.

But she was the only one to blame. I'd offered her a way out—but she didn't take it.

So I took her for myself.

I went outside and grabbed the clothes my men had picked up from the personal shopper. Everything was on hangers and wrapped in a plastic bag. It had to be almost a hundred pounds worth of clothes, but I carried it into the elevator and back into the living room.

Cassini had confined herself to her bedroom most of the time and only came out for meals. She happened to enter the living room at that moment, dressed in my boxers and t-shirt. The clothes were too big, but she somehow made them sexier than lingerie. She was the only woman I'd seen wearing my clothes, and I wouldn't mind if she walked around the house like that all the time.

I laid the clothes across the table. "Here." I pulled the plastic wrapping off the top, revealing jeans, tops, cocktail dresses, and a few formal gowns.

She eyed the pile of clothes then turned back to me. "Let me know how much I owe you."

I admired her pride, but it was useless under my roof. "I'm your owner. I'll take care of you."

Her eyes lit up with the flames of hell. Her lips pursed together tightly like she was trying to control whatever outburst lay behind her lips. Whenever I looked pissed, I looked like an angry god, but when this woman was angry, it only heightened her sex appeal. Whether she was moaning or yelling at me, I found her equally attractive. Right now, she looked like she wanted to slap me hard across the face, just the way she did with Lucian. "Fuck you, you don't own me."

"Change the label if you want, but you can't change the situation." I'd never kept a woman as a prisoner before. I got off on power—but not quite like this. But this was a slight against Lucian as well as a guilty pleasure for me. I had no idea how long I would keep her or what I would do with her, but I knew I wanted her—for as long as she kept my interest. And if she kept looking pissed off like that, I might keep her forever. "Get dressed. We're leaving."

"Where are we going?" The shirt was so loose that one side hung off her shoulder and halfway down her arm. With her gorgeous skin exposed, she was basically asking me to sink my teeth right into her flesh.

"Stop asking questions and get dressed." I wasn't used to someone questioning me left and right. My men did what I said because they believed in my leadership—and they also didn't want to get shot in the foot. But this woman was fearless.

"I'm not a whore who just follows directions."

"Never said you were." I stepped away and made a phone call while she got ready in her bedroom. By the time I was finished, she stepped out in jeans and t-shirt.

"I hope I'm dressed for the occasion..."

She looked fuckable in anything. It was the first time I'd seen her in something other than a dress, and even though the clothing covered her beautiful legs and her shirt wasn't as tight as her dresses, she still made my heart stop for a second. "You could be naked and still be dressed for the occasion."

We left the compound and got into my truck. Then we drove a few blocks away to the doctor's office.

She read the sign out front. "I'm not sick."

"That's not why we're here."

"Then why are we here?"

"We're getting tested."

She turned her head my way, her beautiful brown hair swaying with her movements. She hadn't put on makeup because she hadn't had time, but she was one of the few women in the world who didn't really need it. She had naturally red lips, sexy cheekbones, and green eyes that reminded me of the green valleys of Switzerland in spring. "Does that mean what I think it means?"

I nodded.

"Both of us, right?"

I nodded again.

"What's the point of that if you're sleeping around?"

She continued to make the assumption I'd been with other women when I hadn't. She'd been the only woman in my bed since the night we met. I didn't practice monogamy, but I'd never been with a woman I wanted twice. For some inexplicable reason, I wanted this woman more than twice. More like a million times. But I refused to correct her. "They're also putting a tracker in your ankle. I'll be able to find you anywhere in the world. Not that you would run."

"What makes you think I won't run?" She cocked an eyebrow.

I stared at her, my eyes lingering on the hollow in her throat. "Do you want to go back to Lucian?"

"No, but—"

"I'm the only man in the world who can keep him away from you." If he crossed me, I would enslave him. I would kill all his men, and I would torture him mercilessly. Then I would get everything I wanted.

She shut her mouth, her eyebrow slowly descending. She despised Lucian a lot more than she would ever despise me, and not just because she was fucking me. At least I was a man who could be respected, a man who was strong enough to protect a woman. By my side, she would never have to worry about anything again.

"If you run away and somehow manage to succeed, he'll take you. And what do you think he'll do to you?"

Her face turned noticeably pale.

If he didn't kill her, he would beat her. And death was preferable to being underneath that man every night. Maybe I was an asshole, but at least she liked to fuck me. And at least I was a real man. "Let's go."

NOT THAT I expected anything else, but our results indicated we were both clean. The tracker was successfully placed in her ankle, and the doctor didn't raise any questions to my unusual request. He was the doctor I called in the middle of the night when my men were shot or stabbed. He was paid handsomely under the table, and he looked the other way to all my illegal activities.

We returned to the compound and took the elevator to my floor. I hadn't told my brother what I did because we hadn't crossed paths yet. He was busy working, and I was busy leading.

"You know, I could carve the tracker out of my ankle." She stepped inside the living room and left her shoes by the door, making herself at home already.

As she should. She would live with me for a long time. "You'd probably die."

"It takes a lot more than some pain to kill me."

It was hard not to grin at everything she said. "From the blood loss."

She shrugged. "That still doesn't scare me."

"It's pretty close to a vein, so it should scare you."

The confidence disappeared from her gaze. With her arms crossed over her chest, she walked into the kitchen and looked in the fridge. "Oh, good...you got some food."

"There was already food in there."

"But real food. Like cheese." She grabbed a beer before she came back to me. She held it to her lips and took a long drink while she kept her eyes on me. She sauntered around my living room like she owned it, like she was enticing me with her natural allure. But she wasn't the kind of woman that had to purposely be sexy to seduce a man. She was just naturally magnetic, the way she swayed her hips and sealed her lips around the head of that bottle.

"We have different definitions of food." I didn't really drink beer. The only reason that was in the fridge was because she'd added it to the list. Beer was for pussies, but watching her drink it was a turn-on. I never saw her drink it when we first met, but now that I was getting to know the real her, I realized she preferred it.

"If you're the kind of man that doesn't care about anything, then why be so disciplined?" She sat on the couch and crossed her legs.

"Because a man should be disciplined. I put my life on the line every day. Can I do that if I'm not in the best shape I can possibly be? Women like to get under me for a reason, not just because I'm rich."

"But don't you pay for sex?"

Sometimes I wondered if she was jealous. She mentioned my other hookups often. "I don't pay for sex because I have to. I pay for it because it's easier."

She took a drink of her beer as she stared at me.

I stood in the entryway and loosened my watch from around my wrist. I pulled my gun from the back of my jeans and tossed it on the counter. The ring on my right hand was heavy, but I never took it off. It was much too valuable to leave lying around. "I'm gonna shower, then I'll be gone for most of the evening."

She was about to take a drink, but she lowered the beer back to her thigh. "Where are you going?"

I didn't bother answering her question. I would come and go all the time, and I refused to explain my whereabouts to someone I owned. She had no rights, no opinion. She was like a dog. Her job was to stay home and wait for me to come home. I walked into the hallway.

"Uh, hello?"

I looked at her over my shoulder.

"Are you going to answer me?"

I hardly gave her a glance before I kept walking. "I don't answer anyone. That includes you."

3

BALTO

I sat on my throne with a scotch in my hand. The men drank at the tables around the bar, laughing and talking while the strippers danced around on the stage. Music played over the speakers, and the lights were low. We turned our bar into a trafficking auction one minute and then a strip joint the next.

I puffed on my cigar and felt the burn all the way to my lungs. I was happiest when I had a drink in one hand, a cigar in the other, and a woman on my lap. All I had to do was wave euros in the air and a woman would be at my beck and call. But I already had a woman waiting for me at home.

I didn't owe her anything.

I would never owe her anything.

But after having her bareback, I wanted her even more than before. I didn't want a different woman to ride my dick with a condom minimizing the sensation. I didn't want another woman on me at all—even if she was clean.

"What the hell happened to you?" Heath appeared at

my side, having just walked in with his team. In a dark blue shirt and black jeans, he looked better with every passing week. The scars of jail slowly started to fade away. Like a weed that hadn't had rain in so long, he'd finally quenched his thirst and took over the entire garden. The men didn't struggle to tell us apart, because I had a skull ring and he didn't. That iconic piece of jewelry set us apart. The ring I wore casually on my hand was worth a billion, at the very least. Only a truly brave man would wear it constantly instead of hiding it away.

"Meaning?" I looked at the stripper closest to me on the stage. In nothing but a little black thong, she danced around because she'd been paid a fortune to do so. Anytime we booked them for a wild night, they called in sick at their other gigs and jumped at the chance to entertain us. They were paid handsomely, enough to buy themselves an apartment in the city.

Heath pulled up a wooden chair and sat beside me. The topless bartender put a drink in his hand without even asking him what he wanted. "Thanks, sweetheart." He gave her a playful tap on the ass as she walked away.

She turned around and stabbed him with her eyes. "Look, don't touch. And you better tip me good for that." She flipped her hair and marched off to help the other guys.

She was surrounded by the coldest criminals in the country, but she wasn't afraid to hold her ground. That took balls—the kind of balls I admired. I drank from my glass and continued to watch the stripper, staring at her without really looking at her. Once you'd seen as many tits as I had, they all looked the same. But Cassini had a very impressive rack. She had big tits that were so perfectly shaped, they seemed fake. But I'd squeezed them enough times to know they were real.

After Heath watched the waitress walk away, he turned back to me. "That one's got a bit of an attitude."

"You have to have an attitude if you want to survive around here."

"Definitely." He drank from his glass. "A woman with an attitude turns me on...not sure why."

Same with me. I hadn't noticed it until recently...not until I met Cassini. But no other woman had the nerve to stand up to me. Cassini was a smart woman and knew she was in over her head. That didn't stop her from standing her ground against me. Even if it was pointless, she tried anyway. She hadn't put out yet, but her restraint would wane. Once she was comfortable with her new arrangement, her legs would slowly spread and I would pound her until she was sore.

"So, you didn't get the diamond or the explosives. I'm guessing that's why you look like shit right now."

"I look like shit because I'm talking to you."

Heath cracked a smile. "Always a smartass, huh?"

"Always." I drank my scotch and finally turned to look into his face. "And no, I didn't get either."

"So, are we going to kill him, then?"

"No. We need him alive." Lucian would hide the diamond in a place I would never find it, and if he were dead, he couldn't work for me. I needed him alive—and submissive. "So I took something else."

"Who did you kill this time? I know you wouldn't lay a hand on his wife."

I'd lay two hands on her—on her tits and ass. "I didn't kill anyone. But I took Cassini for my own."

Heath slowly shook his head, a grin on his face. "Bold."

"She's valuable to him, so I know it was a hard blow."

"But is that the real reason you took her?" he challenged. "Or did you do that for yourself?"

I shrugged. "Both. Torture for him, reward for me."

"She must be happy."

"Not so much. She thought I'd rescued her. Then I enlightened her. She simply switched masters—that's all."

"She must prefer you to him."

"I'm sure she does. But she's still pissed." And I liked it when she was pissed. She did this provocative thing with her mouth... I couldn't get enough of it. "Which is fine by me because she's sexy when she's pissed."

"If she's your prisoner, can I get a go?"

I turned my gaze on him, provoked by the question. "Touch her and I'll kill you."

He chuckled then took a drink. "We've shared women before, but this one is off-limits, huh?"

"Yes." I stared him down with my cold eyes, promising a painful death if he disobeyed me.

"Damn. She's a beauty."

"I'll smash this glass over your skull." I lifted my scotch and shook the glass so the ice cubes tapped against the sides.

He brushed off the threat. "I like making you angry. It's so easy."

I turned back to the strippers.

"So, she's just going to live with you?"

"She'll do whatever I want for the foreseeable future."

"And what about when you get bored of her? Can I have her then?"

I assumed I would get bored of her eventually, but I still didn't want to hand her off to my brother. Truth be told, I had no idea what I would do when my boredom descended. I didn't want to give her back to Lucian because I wanted to punish him. But I couldn't let her go because he would find her eventually. The only option I had was to kill her. That seemed like a waste. But that might be the only way to get Lucian to cooperate. That diamond was worth a lot more than her life, but he might have deeper feelings for her. There was no other way to explain his marriage to her. He could have kept her as a slave. He was never obligated to marry her. He did that by his own choosing. "No."

"So even when you don't want her, I still can't have her?" he asked incredulously.

"Let's cross that bridge when we get to it. Calm the fuck down and screw one of the strippers if you're so horny."

"I've been fucking anything and everything since I got out of the joint. But Cassini is fucking exquisite. That dark skin, those luscious lips—"

I slammed the glass against his skull, shattering the tumbler into pieces and sending him to the floor simultaneously.

Everyone in the room stopped and turned at the commotion, seeing my brother lying at my feet with a bleeding head and shards of glass sprinkled across his shirt and pants.

I snapped my fingers, and the waitress instantly put a new drink in my hand. I took a sip and watched the dancers again.

Heath groaned and rubbed his bleeding head. "Be careful, Balto. You only make me want her more."

Without looking at him, I stomped my foot into his knee. "Be careful, Heath. I might actually kill you one of these days."

4

CASSINI

I was alone.

It was the first time I'd ever been truly alone since I married Lucian. Even when he wasn't at the house, Maria and the other staff were there. Armed men were positioned across the grounds, visible out of every window. But since I was on the fourth floor of the building, it was easy to forget about the men guarding the building.

It was three in the morning, and I still couldn't sleep.

I wasn't sure why I was so unnerved. When Balto was down the hall, I slept just fine. But without him there, I somehow felt vulnerable. No one could get past those men and disable the alarm to the elevator to get me, but I still felt exposed.

If Lucian were ever to intercept me, he would punish me. He would punish me for the way I'd slapped him in front of all his men. Then he would punish me for leaving with Balto even though I didn't have a choice. And while this wasn't my fault, he would punish me for sleeping with Balto.

There was a good chance Lucian might kill me.

And if he didn't, he would make my existence so unbearable, I'd wish I were dead.

I could have watched TV in my room, but I decided to grab a beer from the fridge and lie on the couch in the living room. At this hour, there was nothing good on TV, so I watched old reruns of shows that had been off the air for over a decade.

I kept glancing at the time, wondering when he would come home.

What was he doing? Was he out with another woman? I hadn't entered his bed because I was too upset to want him. The man had turned me into a prisoner and bossed me around like I had no rights. Now, he wasn't the sexy stranger I met in a bar, but another asshole who thought he could own me.

But the idea of him being out with someone else got under my skin.

Did he pay for sex? Did he go to one of his whores?

Or was he doing something else? Something criminal?

He didn't tell me anything about his life, so I didn't have a clue. At least with Lucian, I knew exactly where he was and what kind of meeting he was having.

Balto didn't buy me any sleepwear, so I was stuck wearing his stuff. I wondered if he did it on purpose.

At half past four, the cogs in the elevator started to work, and the doors opened a second later. Balto stepped inside dressed in all black. Despite the late hour, there was no hint of his exhaustion. He didn't notice me on the couch because he didn't bother to look. He pulled out his wallet, his keys, and removed his watch. He tossed everything on the entryway table.

My eyes were heavy from exhaustion, and now that he was home, I suddenly felt like I could go to sleep. I wasn't sure if I felt safe because he was here, or I was just relieved that he wasn't out and about.

He stopped when he noticed me. He stilled near the couch, his blue eyes staring at me with pure focus. He didn't blink, turning into a wild animal that watched his prey so carefully. His muscular arms hung by his sides, and his strong chest stretched his cotton t-shirt. He always looked good in black, making his fair skin even more beautiful.

I was in a pair of boxers and a t-shirt without a bra, and even though it wasn't the kind of pajamas I would normally wear, it was the most comfortable clothing I'd ever worn. I sat up on the couch, my hair in a ponytail.

He stepped closer to the couch, still staring at me with predatory eyes. He didn't say a word, choosing to let the silence speak for him.

I spoke first. "You're out late." Accusation was in my voice, even though he didn't owe me anything. Even if I weren't his prisoner, he could come and go as he pleased without explaining his whereabouts. If I had my freedom, I would never tell him about my plans.

"Why are you still awake?"

The bed was comfortable, and I could set the temperature to whatever I wanted. Comfort definitely wasn't the problem. I had no idea what the problem even was. "Couldn't sleep."

"Why is that?"

I held his gaze and didn't come up with an answer.

"My men on the ground are the best I have. They're not gonna let anyone near this building. And even if someone managed to get through, they aren't going to make it up here. So you have nothing to worry about."

That should have eased my mind, but it didn't.

Balto kept watching me. "Not good enough, huh?"

"Are you gone every night?" I couldn't figure out his schedule. He seemed to be out of the house in the evenings, but he left sporadically at all hours of the day.

"Most nights."

I stared into his face and noticed the brightness in his eyes. After a long night doing whatever he did, he didn't appear the least bit tired. It seemed like it was early in the morning and he just woke up from a great night of sleep. "You don't seem tired."

"I don't get tired."

"Well, that's not possible."

"I have too much shit to do to be tired." He stepped away from the couch and entered the kitchen. A cabinet opened and shut, and he poured himself a glass of liquor. He came back to the couch and took a seat beside me.

"What kind of shit are you talking about?"

He stared at the empty fireplace and took a drink.

"Are you never going to tell me about your evenings?"

"I don't see why it matters to you."

"Lucian always told me his plans."

"I'm not Lucian." His tone was ice-cold. "And I don't see why you would want me to be."

"I don't..." Balto claimed to be a cruel man, but he'd never raised a hand to me, and he hadn't forced me to do anything I wasn't comfortable with. He said Lucian wasn't a man at all, that he was a pathetic pussy. But Lucian had been far crueler to me. "You treat me much better than he did."

"How so?" He kept drinking even though he'd probably spent his entire night with a scotch in his hand. "You're my prisoner now. You have no rights, no freedoms. You might not be my wife, but I own you."

Hearing him wrap me in chains disturbed me all the way to my core. I was in this position because of Evan, and now it seemed like I would always be a prisoner. Lucian may have married me, but Evan was the one who had locked the cuffs around my wrists. "You can keep me as your prisoner and take away my freedom—but you'll never own me."

He turned his gaze on me, his blue eyes terrifying.

"A woman can only be owned by a man when she wants to be owned."

He set the glass on the table then continued to watch me. "How do I treat you better?"

"For one, you don't knock me around."

His eyes narrowed slightly, like that statement made him angry. "He hurt you?"

"Sometimes."

He faced forward again. "Just because I haven't laid a hand on you doesn't mean I won't. Just don't give me a reason to, and we won't have a problem."

Maybe he was telling the truth. Maybe he wasn't. I didn't know this man well enough to figure it out. "You haven't forced me to do anything I don't want to do..."

"If you don't cooperate, I will." He turned back to me. "I

will tie your wrists to my headboard and take you however I wish. Maybe I don't own your soul, but I own your body. I will use it however I want."

"And you expect me to just lie there?"

"You did with Lucian."

My eyes lit up in flames. "That was because I had to. With you, I don't owe you anything. I never promised anything to you."

"Submit. Or I will hand you back to Lucian."

My heart gave out in fear because that was the last thing I wanted. But I also knew he took me for a reason. He wanted to punish Lucian for his betrayal, and I was the key to that. "I don't believe you."

He stared me down with that incredible poker face, threatening me with just a look. "It won't come to that anyway. When I want to take you to bed, you'll comply. A kiss here...a touch there...will be enough to make your knees fall open."

Flashbacks of our intense nights together came back to me, causing a shiver to run down my spine in longing. He was the best sex I'd ever had, and I'd missed him the second he was gone. Our circumstances changed when he took me, but my attraction never did. But I refused to want someone who'd enslaved me to torture his enemy. "As a free woman, I'd be in your bed every night. But as a prisoner, I don't find you the least bit attractive."

The corner of his mouth rose in a smile like he didn't believe me at all. "Then why are you sitting on the couch waiting for me to come home?"

"I'm not waiting for you—"

"There's a TV in your room. There's a living area in your

room. There's a spa-size tub with a TV on the wall. There's no reason to lie on this couch in the middle of the night unless you're waiting for the sound of the door."

I shut my mouth because he had me backed into a corner. The second he'd spotted me in the living room, he must have made that assumption, and now he was using it against me.

He continued to stare me down, full of arrogance because he had the upper hand. "There are a few reasons you could be waiting up for me. First, you're scared when I'm not around. Second, you're worried I'm out sleeping around and that pisses you off. Three, you're worried about me and want to make sure I come home at some point. Four, and this is my favorite reason, your pussy misses my dick. So, which is it? It's gotta be one of those reasons—or all the above."

It'd been over a week since he'd snuck into my bedroom and made me explode around his dick so many times. I'd missed him with every passing day until the moment he told me I was his prisoner. I hadn't missed him in that way ever since, but it was only a matter of time before my body's needs caught up with me.

"Answer me." His arm moved over the back of the couch, and he scooted closer to me, bringing his face close to mine. He was close enough for a kiss, but he never leaned in to seal the deal. His eyes were still hostile. "Or I'll assume they all apply."

When he was this close to me, I could smell the booze on his breath and the cigar smoke on his clothes. But the scent I recognized most of all was the aroma of a woman's perfume. Fruity and fragrant, it was undeniable. The scent singed my nose and made my anger rise. "You were with a woman tonight. I can smell it on you."

"So, it's reason number two."

"No. I just don't understand why you'd get both of us checked and then you're sleeping around. Doesn't make any sense."

He ignored my statement. "If it's not reason number two, then which reason is it?"

"You answer me first." The idea of some busty blonde bouncing on his dick pissed me off. Whether she was paid to please him or did it to please herself, it angered me either way. Lucian had his whores, and I never cared. But with Balto, it was a punch in the stomach.

"You never asked me a question."

"Yes, I did. Were you with someone?"

"You never asked. You just assumed." He moved closer to me, his face so close that if he came any nearer, our lips would touch. His eyes were glued to mine, focused and hostile. His muscular body stretched his t-shirt, showing off all the muscles that were hidden from view.

"Answer me." His refusal of transparency only bothered me even more.

"I'll answer you when you answer me. Why are you up all night waiting for me to come home?"

My answer depended on the extent of my curiosity. I could keep this information to myself if I was okay not knowing where he was tonight. But I wanted to know if I was sharing him with someone else, if I was at risk for catching something. I was lucky that Lucian hadn't given me anything, that he actually wore a condom every time he screwed one of his whores. I'd made it this far, so I didn't want to risk catching something now. "One and two..." I was scared without him there to protect me, and I wanted to know if he was bedding other women.

"Which means number three and four apply as well." Triumph was in his eyes.

"I never said three and four."

"If you want me to protect you, then that means you want me to come home safely. And if you're pissed about me screwing someone else, then that means you want me to only screw you. So yes, all the above."

"I never said that."

"You don't have to, baby." His hand moved to my neck and snaked under the fall of my hair. His fingers wrapped around me, and he squeezed me enough so he could feel the pulse in my neck.

I tried not to relax at his touch, even though my body instantly wanted to. I loved it when he touched me like that, like a man possessing a woman. He knew how to be with a woman, how to make her feel like a woman. It wasn't just his kiss and the size of his package. It was his confidence, his focused intensity, and those beautiful eyes. "Your turn."

He cradled my neck and guided my chin up slightly, forcing me to look at him head on. "No. I wasn't with anyone."

"Then why do you smell like perfume?"

Anger slowly inched into his features. "This is something you need to know about me. I'm the kind of man that doesn't give a damn about sparing your feelings. I'm the kind of man so powerful I don't need to employ deception. I'm the kind of man that will talk shit right to your face. I won't bend the truth to make it easier for you to hear. I won't soften a blow so it's less painful to take. I always speak the truth because I don't need to lie. Only cowards and pussies lie. I'm not afraid of anything—especially the truth. So when I say something to you, it's real. Don't. Question. Me." His hand slid out of my hair as he rose to his feet. "I'm going to bed. If you want to fuck, you know where I'll be."

I watched his large shoulders shift slightly as he walked away. His t-shirt stretched across the muscles of his back, hinting at the powerful strength that lay underneath his skin. His shirt was loose around his waist, but I knew exactly how that part of his physique looked. I stayed on the couch and didn't follow him to his bedroom, having too much self-respect to crawl into his bed like nothing happened. I was relieved he hadn't been with another woman, like an enormous weight had been lifted off my chest. He wasn't mine, but for whatever reason, I didn't want him to be anyone else's. Though, just because he hadn't been with someone tonight didn't mean that he hadn't been with someone before, or that he wouldn't be with someone else in the future.

5

CASSINI

W hen I woke up the next day, it was past noon. I didn't get to sleep until five, and since I had nothing to do during the day, I just slept in as long as I wanted. I hopped in the shower and got ready for the day then headed into the kitchen in search of food.

Balto stood in front of the stove, cooking a piece of salmon with asparagus. He wore black sweatpants with workout shoes, and his bare chest and back were slick with sweat. A plastic gallon jug half filled with water was on the counter beside him. His skin was tinted red from all the blood pumping in his veins. Even the back of his neck was coated in sweat. I stood there for a moment and admired him.

He didn't turn around as he addressed me. "Want me to make you some?"

I didn't want a piece of salmon and vegetables. I'd just woken up, so I would probably make a bowl of cereal. "No thanks. How was your workout?"

"Tough as hell." He slid the food onto a plate and left the dirty pan on the stove. When he turned around, his face was free of sweat, probably because he'd wiped it with a towel. "You're welcome to join me."

"Join you in doing what?" I grabbed a bowl from the counter and filled it with cereal.

"Working out."

I added the milk then raised an eyebrow. "Working out at the gym? Or working out by doing something else?"

"I was referring to the gym. But fucking is great exercise too." The corner of his mouth rose in a smile as he grabbed the enormous jug of water. He carried his lunch to the dining room and took a seat.

I sat across from him. "What makes you think I need to go to the gym?" Lucian had told me I was gaining weight even though I thought I looked just fine. Did Balto feel the same way? Was he an asshole who demanded I be a size zero at all times?

"Everyone needs to go to the gym. It doesn't matter how hot you are, the same rules apply to you."

Okay, maybe he didn't think I needed to lose weight. When I listed the things I wanted at the grocery store, he picked them up. He never gave me shit about my diet. I ate cereal in the morning, a sandwich for lunch, and cookies for dessert. "Why is that?"

"Cardiovascular health. Muscle strength. Stress." He pressed the side of his fork into his fish and shaved off a piece of meat before he popped it into his mouth. "The list goes on." His chest was shiny from the sweat that seeped out through his skin. His muscles seemed a bit bigger because of all the weight lifting he did. It was no surprise he was in such phenomenal shape considering how committed he was to fitness. His size, strength, and discipline definitely made him intimidating.

"Weight loss?" I asked, my eyes directed into my bowl.

"Weight loss shouldn't be your motivation for a healthy lifestyle. And you don't need to lose weight."

I looked up, surprised by what he'd said since Lucian had the exact opposite opinion. "You see what I eat all day."

He shrugged. "Some people can eat whatever they want and look great. Others can't."

"And you think I'm one of those people?" I asked incredulously. I was aware of the thickness of my thighs, of the way my stomach protruded slightly over my jeans. I'd gained weight since I'd lived with Lucian, and that was mainly out of depression. I used to be a lot more active. Now I wasn't active at all.

"Yes." His eyes were locked on mine as he placed a piece of salmon in his mouth.

"Have you not noticed my curves? The way my thighs stretch my jeans?"

"Have you not noticed how hard I get when I'm inside you?" He said the words without skipping a beat, his eyes locked on mine as he continued to chew his food. "Women are different from men. Men should be fit, lean, and strong. They're the protectors, the providers. Women have no such obligation. Their only job is to be healthy and bear children. They can do that at any size."

Maybe I didn't despise him so much, after all. "Lucian told me to lose weight."

He cut his fork into his fish but didn't take a bite. He lifted his gaze to look at me, the sweat slowly evaporating from his fair skin. "He's the one who needs to hit the gym, not you. The guy is a scrawny bastard who makes bombs because he can't throw a punch." He placed the food in his mouth.

Maria had only made me certain meals, stuff that was low in carbs and low in fat, under Lucian's orders. It was ironic because he ate whatever he wanted without considering his health. That was one of the reasons living with Balto was preferable—because I could eat whatever I wanted.

Balto finished everything on his plate then stared at me.

I kept eating my cereal, ignoring his intense expression.

"Why didn't you come to my room last night?"

Bumps formed along my skin, and my hair stood on end slightly. The thought had crossed my mind, but I was too proud to follow through on it. "Did I say I was going to?"

"No. But you wanted to."

"I don't remember saying that."

"I remember you having a hissy fit when you thought I slept with someone else. So why didn't you crawl on my lap and claim me as your own?" He rested his elbows on the table and stared at me, reading my face for an answer.

"Because I didn't want to."

He smiled slightly, like he saw right through my bull-shit. "Right..."

"I didn't."

"Whatever you say, baby. All I have to do is look for

your panties from yesterday in the hamper, and that'll tell me everything I need to know."

I stopped the alarm from sinking into my features so he wouldn't see my fluster—that was the last thing I needed.

"Don't worry. I won't do it. It's not like I need to…"

"Fuck you." I rolled my eyes and looked at my cereal again. "You may think your arrogance is charming, but it's just repulsive."

"How about we look at your current panties and see if that's true?"

I grabbed my bowl and prepared to throw the milk and cereal bits in his face.

With lightning speed, he grabbed my wrists and took the bowl without spilling a drop. He set it beside him at his end of the table. "I don't mind back talk, but I'm not letting you throw milk on me in my own fucking home. Looks like you lost your breakfast."

I threw the spoon at him.

He caught it with his perfect reflexes and tossed it into the bowl. "I understand why you're trying to fight it, but just let it go. We both know what's going to happen. And keep in mind that it's in your best interest to be valuable to me. As long as you're important, I'll keep you around. Be the woman in my bed, be my fantasy, and you'll be the most protected woman in the world. Get on my good side, and you'll have the freedom you used to have. You can do whatever the hell you want, whenever you want. But if I lose interest, I'll have no use for you. So I'll either dump you on the street or kill you just to torture Lucian. You don't want that, right?"

"Did you just threaten me?"

"No. I told you what would happen if you become useless. It's a prediction, not a threat."

"You'd kill an innocent woman?" I asked incredulously.

"I'm keeping you as a prisoner, aren't I? There's no line I won't cross, baby. I suggest you don't test me."

He called me baby but then threatened to kill me. He tried to convince me to be submissive in exchange for a better life. This guy was one arrogant son of a bitch. "You said if I didn't cooperate, you would force me. So why don't you just force me?"

"Do you want me to force you?" His voice deepened with intrigue. The average person blinked several times a minute, but this man hardly blinked at all. At any time, he was still like a statue, an enigma. Like a sponge, he absorbed everything around him, but he dried up so quickly, you couldn't squeeze anything back out. "I don't need to force you because I know you want it. I want what we had, exactly as it was. So I will wait until your aching pussy drives you so crazy, you can't resist any longer."

"You flatter yourself."

"How about I stick two fingers inside you and really flatter myself?"

This man truly had no boundaries.

"You told me that you wished your life could be different. That you could be your own woman and sleep with whomever you wanted. I've given you that life. You can have anything you want, and you can sleep with the only man you want. You can be the most protected woman in the world and have the power to do whatever you want. All you have to do is stop fighting me and embrace it."

"I told you I was a fighter—through and through."

"Then be prepared to accept the consequences of your actions." He rose to his feet and carried the dishes into the kitchen.

I stayed at the kitchen table and thought about the last threat he issued. I wanted to think he was bluffing, but he claimed he never lied. He wanted me to make Lucian suffer, and if Balto wasn't fucking me, then he would have to get his revenge some other way. He'd killed Lucian's brother... so would he kill me too?

After he rinsed the dishes, he left the kitchen and walked past me without a second glance.

My back was turned to him so I couldn't see his expression. "What do you want from me?"

His feet stopped on the hardwood floor.

I stared out the floor-to-ceiling window that overlooked the city. "What's the point in all this?"

He slowly walked back toward me, his footsteps getting louder as he approached me from behind. His scent entered my nose once he was directly behind my chair. His hand slid under the back of my hair, and he gripped my neck, a hint of possessiveness in his fingertips. "I like to torture my enemies, and there are several ways to do that. You can start cutting off fingers and toes, or you could do something more extreme, like psychological warfare. I want Lucian to suffer every single day as he wonders what I'm doing to you, if I'm fucking you in the mouth, pussy, or ass. I want him to be humiliated every time I step out in public with you, when the world knows what I took from him without fear. Eventually, he might try to get you back. When he does, I can let you go for a price. Or I can cross him the way he crossed me and shoot you in the back of the head once he fulfills his end of the bargain. I already enjoy fucking you, beat off to you, so I suggest you become so valuable, so irreplaceable that you're worth more than that fucking diamond and his weapons. Otherwise, you'll end up back where you started...or dead."

6

BALTO

I sat in the dimly lit room with my drink resting on the table in front of me. The strip joint was quiet tonight, probably because it was almost two in the morning on a Wednesday. The only men in the place were pathetic ones who had nowhere else to go—and criminals that never slept.

Heath sat in the back, a gun tucked under his jacket. He had me in his line of sight in case this meeting went to shit.

Finally, the man I was meeting made his move. He sat in the chair beside me, a cigar in his mouth and a drink in his hand. He blew out the smoke as he stared at the girls as they spun on their poles with their tits hanging out. A noticeable scar stretched from the top of his hand up his forearm. It was clearly a stab wound. Someone had pierced him with a knife and dragged the blade all the way to his elbow, skinning him like an animal after a hunt. "Hunter Reyes is undercutting you. He's got a lot more money pouring in than he reports. He's not just skimming off the top. We're talking big money here."

"Proof?" I couldn't torture and kill a man without being certain. The world respected me because I was fair and just. Only if you were truly guilty would you be put to death. If I killed an innocent man, it would make me seem stupid and careless. Men believed in my verdicts, so they had to always be accurate. Besides, I didn't want to kill a man who made me money.

"I don't have any. It's just what I've seen."

It was hard to get proof without sticking out your neck too far. When my spies reported information to me, I knew they were legitimate. They couldn't always provide me paperwork, photos, or recordings, but that didn't make it untrue. "I'll look into it." All I had to do was stop by unexpectedly and take a look myself. If I found something, I'd finish the job then and there. If I didn't find something, it would scare them so much they would take advantage of their second chance to do the right thing. "How much is he skimming?"

"I know he bagged ten during his last deal. But he only reported five."

Hunter did only report five, so that made my spy more credible. I pulled out the wad of cash and set it on the table. "Leave."

He stuffed the money into his jacket then left the strip club.

I stared straight ahead and looked at the girls without paying attention to them. My thoughts were focused entirely on Hunter Reyes, head of one of my biggest drug cartels. He pulled in money from the eastern countries. He had the most connections and the most men, so he was able to produce his product very quickly. The Cardello brothers were becoming the next biggest competitors with their amazing product. Case Cardello appeared fearless, but he didn't seem stupid enough to cross me.

A woman emerged from the rear then took the seat beside me. In a dress that was so short it barely covered her thong, she was dressed for attention. Her hand snaked up my arm and rubbed my bicep as she leaned close to me. "Balto seems tense."

I recognized her voice along with her deep brown hair. "It's been a long night."

She leaned in closer to me and pressed a kiss to my neck. "Let's make it even longer."

Yvonne was one of my regular whores. She knew exactly what I liked and charged a fortune for it. I kept my hands to myself and my dick in my pants even though it'd been almost two weeks since I'd been buried in pussy. I knew Cassini would open her legs eventually, either out of desire or obligation. "Not tonight, Yvonne." I gently slid her hand off my bicep.

She pouted her lips. "You definitely seem stressed. Nothing a blow job can't fix."

I used to be attracted to Yvonne, but now my dick didn't come out to play. My sex drive was fueled toward a single woman, the wife of one of my biggest enemies. I wanted to be buried balls deep inside her and pumping her with my come. Sex with someone else would feel stale and unsatisfying. "Not tonight."

She raised an eyebrow. "I've never heard you say no before."

I turned to her, my anger starting to rise. "I'm saying it now. Goodnight, Yvonne."

"Alright...asshole." She left my side and disappeared into the darkness of the club.

I drank from my glass and kept watching the girls.

Heath fell into the chair beside me moments later. "How'd it go?"

"Hunter Reyes is lying about his profits."

"By how much?"

"Half."

Heath shook his head. "That fucker is gonna die."

"Along with a few other people."

Heath stared at the girls before he glanced over his shoulder and looked into the darkness. "Who was that fine woman in the black dress?"

"One of my whores."

"Really? Is she off-limits too?"

"No." I couldn't complain about double-dipping with a whore. It was how she made her living. Heath and I had fucked the same woman before, so it wasn't surprising. Cassini was different on infinite levels.

"Good. What's her price range?"

"She's expensive—but worth it."

"It looked like you turned her down."

"Because I did."

Heath drank from his glass then looked at me. "Because your little prisoner is more than you can handle?"

"No. She's not sleeping with me."

"Really? Why not?"

"Because she's pissed at me." The sex we used to have was so earth-shattering that the ground shook beneath my feet. She was so enthusiastic, releasing all her sexual frustrations with my body on top of hers. She fucked me like it was all she needed to live. I was the one thing she looked forward to in life, the one guilty pleasure that brought her joy. But all of that disappeared once I took her prisoner. I knew she still wanted me, but she was just too stubborn to act on it.

"Who gives a damn if she's pissed? She's your prisoner —and she has a job to do."

The idea of forcing her got my dick hard, but I preferred the affectionate and obsessive woman I used to bed. She grabbed my ass and pulled me deeper inside her even though she could barely take all of me. I wanted that woman, that passion and heat. "She'll come around."

"But you shouldn't have to wait. And in the meantime... there's a fine piece of ass that wants you right over there."

She only wanted me because I paid her a fortune in cash. "Take her, Heath."

"You're the one not getting laid. I'm doing you a favor."

"Don't worry about my dick. Worry about your own."

"Whatever, man." He finished off his drink. "Just trying to help."

"Don't."

"So when are we going to move against Hunter?"

"Sometime this week. We'll ambush him. If I give him any kind of warning, he can prepare for the conversation. The best time to read someone is during that first interaction, and I can't read him over the phone."

"You want me to tag along?"

"I'm trying to keep our resemblance a secret."

"Why is that?" Heath watched the naked women dance around, their cleavage pressed against the poles and their asses barely covered in their thongs.

"It might be useful down the road."

"Does Cassini know?"

I shook my head. She knew I had a brother, but she didn't know I was a twin.

"Lucian contacted you?"

"Nope." He was too much of a pussy to move against me. If he didn't agree to meet my demands, he would never get his wife back. So unless he was prepared to go to war with me, there was nothing he could do. He might have the explosives to destroy an entire city, but I had an army that could destroy the entire world. He might be a stupid man, but he wasn't that stupid. He'd have to methodically plan his advance before he did a damn thing.

"You think he will?"

"Eventually. He'll negotiate to get Cassini back."

"And will you give her back?"

"Depends."

"On what, exactly?" he asked.

"What he's offering. And how valuable she becomes."

I STEPPED off the elevator at four in the morning. My pockets were emptied, and my valuables were placed on the entryway table. My eyes turned to the couch, wondering if Cassini would be there like last time.

She was.

She'd been asleep just a minute ago, but the sound of the elevator stirred her. She'd been waiting for that beep to tell her I was home, and now that I was in the building, she could relax.

I walked over to the couch, a gloating smile on my face. This woman had only been here for a short time, but she was already dependent on me in many ways. Clearly, I made her feel safe because the second I was gone, she was uncomfortable. Knowing she needed me for something was a turn-on, especially when she tried to pretend that wasn't true.

She sat up and tucked her hair behind her ear, her eyes heavy from exhaustion as well as the rest she'd just had. She looked at me before she looked away, clearly ashamed by my arrogant smile. "I fell asleep watching TV. I wasn't—"

"Liar." I looked at her baggy t-shirt and boxers and wished I could rip them both off. My dick seemed to always be hard around her because I'd been unsatisfied for so long. Jerking off wasn't cutting it. I'd never been a fan of masturbation in the first place. I'd always preferred real pussy to the imaginary pussy I could replicate with my hand.

I scooped my arms underneath her body and lifted her from the couch. Light as a feather and with the softest skin, she was a perfect fit in my arms. I cradled her against my chest then carried her down the hallway, feeling her body heat against mine.

Her arm immediately circled my neck as a flash of surprise crossed her face. But she allowed me to carry her down the hallway and into her bedroom. Her eyes moved to my neck before they narrowed.

I set her on the bed then straightened, hoping she would invite me between her legs. But when I saw the pissed-off look on her face, I knew that wasn't going to happen.

"Out with one of your whores tonight?" She scooted away from me until she was in the center of the bed.

My head cocked slightly at the accusation.

"Don't give me that bullshit speech about your integrity. I can see the damn lipstick all over your neck." She scooted back against the headboard, trying to get as far away from me as possible. "If you think I'm going to fuck you without a condom when you're screwing whores, then forget it."

I recalled the moment Yvonne kissed me on the neck. Her bright-red lipstick probably smeared against my neck, and now it marked me like a tattoo. My fingers reached up and brushed the area. When I stared at my hand, I could see the paint on my skin.

She rolled her eyes. "Say what you want about Lucian, but at least he didn't pretend to be something he wasn't."

I didn't want to be compared to that man, especially when he was painted in a better light. "I didn't sleep with anyone tonight."

She rolled her eyes. "I don't believe you."

I was annoyed she didn't believe me like everyone else, but her jealousy was entertaining. She didn't like the idea of me being buried between another woman's legs—at all. "I was at a strip club tonight."

She slowly turned back to me, her arms crossed over her chest.

"I met with one of my spies. He informed me that one of my drug dealers isn't fairly distributing his profits. When he left, one of my regular whores came over. She snuggled into my side, kissed me on the neck, and offered to suck me off. I turned her down."

Cassini kept staring at me, the rage burning like a bonfire.

"Then I came home."

"You expect me to believe that—"

"I don't give a damn if you do. In fact, watching the jealousy torment you is very entertaining. If you want me all to yourself, then take me. You want my fidelity? Then ask for it. We both know you want it."

She looked away, her arms tightening over her chest.

"If you don't want another woman to fuck me, then you better start riding my dick. A man can't be tempted when he's satisfied. That's my best advice to you."

"Get out." Her voice came out weak, like she lost her fire.

I wanted to confess that she was the only woman I'd been with since the night we met. My cock hadn't been tempted by anyone else because she was all I wanted. But that information would give her too much power. I would much rather hear her demand my monogamy than freely give it to her. Much sexier that way. "Whatever you say, baby." I moved to the door.

"I'm not your baby. Don't call me that."

"If you weren't my baby, you wouldn't get pissed off by another woman's lipstick. So yes, you are my baby—whether you like it or not."

7

CASSINI

W hen I saw that lipstick on his neck, I flipped a switch.

Imagining some woman dragging her tongue up and down his body pissed me off. I was sleeping on the couch waiting for him to come home while some other woman was sinking her claws into him.

I shouldn't care, but I wasn't going to pretend that I didn't.

He said nothing happened, but I didn't know if I could believe him. He was a man of his word, a man who wasn't afraid to do whatever he wanted. He snuck into Lucian's house to fuck me without caring about getting caught. He didn't care about anything. So why should he care about being with other women? Why would he lie? I was his prisoner regardless of whether or not he pissed me off. Whether or not there were other women in his bed didn't change the fact that I belonged to him.

I was angry with him anyway. I believed him the first

time, but the sight of that lipstick made my skin burn like it was on fire.

I didn't leave my room the entire day because I didn't want to see his face. I didn't want to look at those pretty blue eyes and that handsome face, not when they might soften my anger.

I hadn't had a phone in almost two weeks, and I hadn't checked in with my brothers. If I went too long without contacting them, they would really start to worry. I needed to negotiate some kind of freedom soon—and I suspected that meant I had to sleep with him. If I ever wanted to leave this building, I would have to give in.

At three in the afternoon, there was a knock on my door.

I refused to open it. "Go away."

The sound of something solid tapped against the hard-wood floor on the other side of the door. The clatter of utensils followed. His footsteps sounded again a second later, retreating as he moved back down the hallway and into the living room.

My curiosity got the best of me, so I opened the door.

On the ground was a plate of food. A turkey sandwich with a bag of chips and a pickle. There was a cold bottle of beer and a glass of water too. The sight softened my heart just a little, but I took a deep breath and tried to brush it off.

I took everything into my room and ate, comforting my starving belly with food. I ate the entire bag of chips and downed the beer like water. A slight headache formed at the front of my right temple because I'd fasted for too long.

I finished everything and left the plate on the coffee

table. I still refused to leave the room, so I took a bath then read for a few hours. After a late afternoon nap, night fell.

He knocked on my door again, close to eight in the evening.

I didn't open it. "What?"

"I'm leaving for the night."

Disappointment washed through me. He seemed to be gone most evenings. When we were sleeping together, he always seemed to be home, but he must have changed his schedule so he could be with me then.

He set something on the ground. "I got you a phone. My number is in your phone book if you need me."

"What if I call the cops? Tell my family?"

He chuckled in his deep voice. "You do that, baby." His footsteps sounded as he walked off.

I wondered if he would come home with lipstick on his neck again. Was he going out for work? Or was he hooking up with someone? I'd never cared who Lucian was screwing, but I couldn't fight the pain and jealousy when I imagined Balto coming inside someone else. It haunted me.

But I refused to vocalize my thoughts. I refused to share my vulnerability. Even if he already knew how I felt, I refused to confirm it. As a Cardello, I was much too stubborn. That would only mean I actually had feelings for this man, feelings for the man who had captured me like I was an animal rather than a person. So I would stick to my guns...as long as possible.

JUST LIKE EVERY OTHER NIGHT, I couldn't sleep.

I paced around the floor and looked out the window, seeing the city lights and the streets I used to frequent all the time. It'd been so long since I lived a normal life that I could barely remember how that used to be. I'd lived in a little apartment in the city, and Evan slept over all the time. We would cook dinner every night, make love, and then he would leave for work in the morning.

Then everything changed.

My life had never been the same.

Living with Lucian was straightforward because I knew exactly how I felt about the situation. But living with Balto was much more confusing. I was attracted to the man, more attracted to him than I'd ever been to anyone else. The second I saw him in that bar, my heart skipped a beat. When he left food outside my door, I couldn't help but think it was sweet. He could have ordered me to come out or dragged me by the hair. Lucian slugged me in the stomach, but I couldn't imagine Balto treating me that way—even if he was the more dangerous man.

I moved into the kitchen and grabbed a few cookies before I made my way to the couch. It was midnight, so he wouldn't be home for hours. My ears focused on every little sound I heard throughout the floor. I didn't believe someone could manage to make it up the elevator to me, but sometimes I feared Lucian would line the building with explosives and detonate it. I would die from the explosion or be buried under the rubble of the building. Having Balto there couldn't prevent that, but it made me feel safer anyway.

There was something about that man that made me feel untouchable.

I'd never seen a man stand up to Lucian so effortlessly, let alone twice. He'd burned a cigar into his hand without retaliation. He'd shown up at his home and took me like a product off the shelf at a grocery store. This man had unquestionable power, and I had to admit it made me feel invincible.

But when he wasn't around, I felt powerless.

Vulnerable.

Afraid.

I turned on the TV and pulled a blanket over my shoulders. My beer sat on the coffee table untouched, and my eyes grew heavy from the late hour. I wanted to hear the elevator the second he came home, and I wouldn't be able to do that in my room. It took a while for my brain to finally drift off to sleep, and when I did, I started to dream.

And I dreamed of my captor.

As if I was back in time, I was in my old bedroom at Lucian's. It was dark because it was late in the evening, but I wasn't alone.

Balto peeled off all my clothes and gave me a look of such possessiveness that I didn't feel like a married woman anymore. My ring was gone because I belonged to him exclusively. His massive body dipped the bed as he moved on top of me, all muscle and beautiful skin. His sculpted thighs separated mine, and he shoved his large size inside me, our bodies skin-to-skin.

"Balto..." I felt the goodness between my legs, the fullness every woman should feel when they were with a man. My nipples dragged against his chest as he moved with me, the sweat starting to slicken both our bodies. My arms circled his neck, and I kissed him as I felt him inside me, my body tensing and tightening in preparation for another climax. I buried my face in his shoulder and felt my teeth drag against his collarbone as I did my best to keep quiet. Another man was pleasing me, and I didn't want my husband to overhear. It was just like the last night we were together, our passion hotter than an inferno. My ankles locked together around his waist because I never wanted him to leave.

I was pulled from my dreams when I felt my hips being dragged across the couch. My boxers were yanked off my long legs, and the blanket that had been on top of me was absent. My eyes snapped open in alarm, and that's when I saw Balto, gloriously naked. His enormous cock was at full mast and ready to pound into me.

He moved on top of me and hooked his arms behind my knees. "Miss me, baby?" He smothered me into the cushions and pressed his crown against my entrance. After a gentle thrust, he pushed inside, becoming smeared in the arousal that was flooding from my body. "Fuck yes, you did." He sank inside me slowly, sliding so perfectly because I was slicker than I'd ever been. He moaned from deep within his throat, getting every single inch inside me until his balls tapped against my skin.

I'd just woken up and couldn't distinguish dream from reality. I was just at Lucian's house a moment ago, this man deep between my legs. Now I was back in reality, sleeping on the couch and waiting for Balto to come home. His cock inside me felt better than the dream, and I was so hard up that I didn't stop him. My hands slid up his chest, and I widened my legs farther to give him complete access.

Skin-to-skin, I felt the incredible sensations, just as I

did the last time we were together. I looked forward to the finale, when my cunt would be stuffed with this man's come. The lipstick on his neck became an afterthought, along with my imprisonment.

He thrust into me while keeping my legs pinned back, our limbs a tangled mess as we screwed on the couch. He didn't just fuck me, but he got his dick deep inside me with every thrust. All he wanted was to feel me, to glide through my tightness because he forgot how good it felt. He stared down at me with a clenched jaw, the moans uncontrollable. He was coming apart right before my eyes, too weak to fight the goodness between my legs. "Jesus Christ…I can't believe you made me wait so long."

I held on to his lower back and pulled myself back into him. His body ground against my clit, and his dick stretched me wide apart. My breathing hitched as my body tensed. All the muscles in my back shivered as I prepared for the orgasm that would make my toes curl. My fingers dug into his ass, and I yanked on him harder. "Balto…" I bit my lip as the climax hit me like a ton of bricks. It was so good, it was actually painful. My pussy struggled to contract because it seemed to have forgotten how. A low moan turned into a scream, and then I pulled on him harder because I wanted every inch of that dick. "Yes…" Both of my toes cramped, but that didn't stop me from enjoying the greatest euphoria of my life. Now I was wide awake, drunk on the pleasure this man gave me.

"Fuck…" He pressed his forehead to mine and gave his final thrusts, pushing his body deep into mine so he could give me every single drop of his arousal. He was usually quiet when he climaxed, but now he was vocal in his pleasure. His hand snaked into my hair as he gave another grunt. "Baby..." Even when he finished, he kept rocking, like he didn't want it to end just yet.

Now that the pleasure had passed, reality hit me hard. I'd given in to my desire and fucked this man as hard as he fucked me. Truth be told, I missed it so much. I missed the intimacy, the connection. Maybe it was just sex, but it was the strongest human relationship I'd had in years. It was a way for me to vent my frustrations, a way for me to feel like a beautiful woman with needs. He was still an escape— even if he was my prison.

Instead of softening like usual, he stayed hard inside me. "Damn, he missed you."

I was soaking wet, so we both knew I missed him.

"Was that better than your dream?"

The desire I'd felt just a second ago evaporated. How did he know I was dreaming about him?

He lifted me from the couch while staying deep inside me and carried me down the hallway and into his bedroom. His eyes were on me, full of that obnoxious arrogance that pissed me off. "You were bucking your hips and whispering my name."

Embarrassment flooded my veins, but I refused to show it on my face. I had no control over my subconscious, over the internal desires that needed to be fulfilled. There was no other man in the world I would ever fantasize about. My list of lovers wasn't long—and Balto was at the top of the list. "Shut up and fuck me." I moved to my hands and knees on the bed so I could enjoy the sex without having to see that stupid smirk on his face. It didn't matter what position he took me in, I always came.

He grabbed my hips and rolled me to my back. "No. I want to look at you."

"Well, I don't want to look at you—"

He silenced my outburst with a kiss, a soft kiss that was purposeful and slow. He held his strong body on top of mine and slowly positioned himself between my legs. His wet cock pressed into my lower lips, and he applied gentle pressure right against my clit. His soft lips moved with mine, instilling the same desire within me just by touch. His mouth moved a little faster, picking up the pace for both of us. His mouth opened, closed, and then opened again, breathing out gentle breaths across my mouth. He sucked my bottom lip before his tongue moved into my mouth and greeted mine in an erotic dance. Slowly, it moved, embracing the inside of my mouth with a kiss so sexy my thighs squeezed against his hips.

He was one hell of a kisser.

His arms locked behind my knees just as they did on the couch, and without breaking our kiss, he tilted his hips and gently sank inside me.

I moaned like it was the first time, like he hadn't just made me come in the living room.

He slid inside me perfectly, moving until his fat dick was exactly where it belonged. His kiss continued, passionate and sexy. His cock throbbed inside me as he forced both of us to wait before the fucking began. "You want to be the only woman who gets my dick?" He pulled back slightly so our eyes could meet.

My hands felt the muscles of his stomach and chest, and I was so buried in sex that I couldn't think clearly. Being with him was when I felt most alive, when life was worth living. The experience wasn't just passionate, but spiritual. I could feel heaven from my scalp to my toes.

"Baby." He slowly pressed into me, making me feel the extent of his enormity. He was so big that he could barely fit inside me, that his crown tapped against my cervix painfully if he pushed too far.

I'd hated seeing the lipstick on his neck. I hated wondering what he was doing while he was out so late. I hated the idea of sharing him with someone else, whether it was a whore or not. "I hate you…" This man was just as evil as Lucian for keeping me as a prisoner. I was locked away in a tower with no rights. He was dangerous, criminal, and lethal. I wanted a normal life with a normal man, but this was what I got.

His eyes narrowed as he stayed deep inside me.

"But I don't want to share you with anyone else…" Shame reverberated through me, cascades of embarrassment and humiliation. I asked for his fidelity, for his monogamy. I was possessive over a man I didn't even like. It was a twisted feeling, so convoluted it was disgusting.

Normally, he would have worn that boyish smile, the one where the corner of his mouth rose in a grin. It would shine in his eyes too, his mirth at my conformity. This time, he didn't display his typical arrogance. His eyes deepened as they locked on mine, desire and lust heavy in the expression. Instead of triumphant, he seemed aroused. It wasn't a victory for his ego, only his dick. "I don't like to share either."

8

BALTO

When I woke up the next morning, I was noticeably warmer than usual. I was aware of the subtle weight on my chest, the slender woman who used my frame as a mattress instead of the bed. My eyes opened, and I remained still so I wouldn't disturb her.

On her stomach with her hair across my shoulder lay Cassini. She was naked underneath the sheets, and the muscles of my body kept her warm throughout the night. She seemed perfectly comfortable even though she was lying on solid rock.

It was the first time I'd woken up to a woman hogging me like that. Women never slept over, and if they did, they stuck to their side of the bed. There was no touching unless it was during sex. But this woman took all of my personal space for herself.

I didn't mind it.

I liked the way she smelled. I liked the way her soft skin felt against mine. I liked the way her hair lightly tickled me whenever she moved. My arm was hooked around the small of her back, and I loved how deep the curve was. This woman was all curves from head to toe, but I particularly liked that one most of all.

She was perfect.

Lucian said she needed to lose weight. That only proved my theory—he was a spineless scumbag. Who said that to their wife? What kind of man said that to any woman? Especially when it couldn't be further from the truth. I liked her thighs. I liked the curve at the bottom of her stomach. I'd never been attracted to women who were exceptionally skinny. If they were skin and bones, I wasn't interested. Despite the fact that I was in great shape, I didn't find fitness attractive in women. Call me old-fashioned, but I liked a woman with an ass, tits, and a belly. Curves were the distinguishable feature in a woman, the epitome of sexuality. If Lucian couldn't appreciate this beautiful woman for all that she was, there was something seriously wrong with him.

It didn't matter anymore. She was mine now.

Listening to her ask me to be hers exclusively was the biggest turn-on. It was sexier than all the dancers at the strip club, sexier than all the kinky shit I did in my lifetime. Listening to this drop-dead gorgeous woman want me all to herself...was something I could beat off to for the rest of my life.

Thankfully, I didn't have to.

She would sleep for several hours, so I carefully rolled her to her back and slowly moved away. The sheets fell slightly, exposing the tops of her tits to the nipples.

I stared at her and debated fucking her, whether she

was conscious or not. But I knew I needed to get my day started. And I knew she would be there waiting for me when I was finished. I got dressed and headed to the gym.

The gym was on the bottom floor, so I took the elevator down and stepped into the weight room.

Heath was there, using the barbell to work on his chest. Two hundred pounds was on the bar, and he finished his reps quickly.

"I hope that's just a warm-up."

Heath racked the bar then sat up. "Shut up, asshole."

I set my jug of water on the counter and grabbed the weights I wanted to use. I hit the gym every single day religiously because my life depended on it. Respect was much easier to garner if I was a fighting machine. I could intimidate anyone with just my appearance. I could get anyone to fuck me with just my appearance too. Cassini didn't want to share me for a reason.

"You seem to be in a good mood."

I did three sets of bicep curls. "Sarcasm?"

"No."

"What makes you think I'm in a good mood?" I did another set then started shoulder presses.

"Because you don't look like shit."

"I never look like shit." I pumped out the reps then racked the weights.

"Trust me, you do." He grabbed his bottle of water and took a drink. "I know you didn't change your mind about Yvonne because I took her home last night. Best two thousand euros I've ever spent. She can take big dick in the ass like a pro."

That was information I didn't need to know. "Just like you did in prison?"

His smile dropped. "I'll throw a weight plate at your head."

"Like you could lift it."

Heath's anger slowly faded away. "See? You're in a really good mood."

"Because I'm talking shit?"

"No. Because you're making jokes. Last night, you were a little girl with her panties up her ass. Your jaw was clenched so tight, and you looked like you wanted to strangle someone."

"Well, you were sitting beside me...maybe I wanted to strangle you."

He studied me for a while, as if he were trying to read the look on my face. "Get laid?"

All night long. "Fuck off, Heath."

The corner of his mouth rose in a smile, just the way mine did. "She finally put out? Took her long enough. Or did you force her?"

I'd never forced a woman in my life. I didn't need to force a woman to get laid. Only men like Lucian did. "Your question is offensive."

"Which one?"

"All of them." I grabbed my earbuds. "I'm tuning you out so I can get something done."

"So you can hurry home and get laid again?"

I popped the buds into my ears and let the music drown out his voice.

WHEN I GOT out of the shower, she was still asleep.

Was she ever going to wake up?

I pulled on my boxers then stared at her, seeing the way she stretched out across my bed and managed to take up the entire thing. She seemed to be reaching for me, and when she couldn't find me, she kept stretching.

Staring at her got me hard, so I dropped the boxers I'd just put on and got into bed with her. She was on her stomach, so my hand palmed her ass and I pressed a kiss to the nape of her neck. Slowly, I kissed her along the spine as my fingers moved to her entrance just below her asshole. They gently made their way inside, getting through her tight entrance and finding the wetness that always greeted me. I could feel my come inside her too, sticky and warm. My fingers pulsed as I kissed her.

She moaned with her eyes closed, and slowly the pleasure forced her to wake. Her eyes opened, and she looked at me over her shoulder, her pussy immediately tightening when she was aware of my fingers. "Not a bad way to wake up…"

"Get used to it." I pulled my fingers out of her cunt then moved on top of her. She was flat on her belly so I couldn't see her tits, but my dick was rock hard because of her beautiful face. I directed my head inside her and slowly sank in, her asshole just a few inches above. When I was deep inside, the most sensual shiver ran all the way down my spine. There was nothing better in life than being balls deep in this pussy. Money was irrelevant, power was overrated. This was true bliss—fucking this woman.

My hand fisted her hair, and I yanked her head back, keeping her spine curved at a sexy angle. Then I turned her head to the side so I could seal my mouth over hers. I kissed her as my hips thrust into her hard, hitting all her slickness deep.

She moaned against my mouth and could barely return my kiss. She was falling apart right off the bat, the pleasure between her legs so good that she couldn't focus on anything else.

I'd missed her pussy so much. Two weeks was my longest drought, and she'd made it an unbearable two weeks. After I had her bare pussy in Lucian's home, I couldn't keep sharing her with the asshole. I wanted to pump my come deep inside her every single night—without sharing. My dick was obsessed with her perfection, with how unnaturally wet she was. Anytime I went anywhere near her pussy, she was practically dripping. A woman had never been so wet, and seeing how aroused she was only turned me on more. She swallowed those olives at the bar like she wished they were my balls. She had the appetite of a whore but the class of a queen.

I pushed her hard against the bed and made her clit drag against the sheets. My hands were balled into fists against the mattress, and I used my ass muscles to really get inside her. At this angle, it was so easy to hit her deep, to feel her at a better angle.

She came a second later, so she must have liked it too. She came against my mouth, her kiss absent because all she could do was moan. Her nails clawed at the sheets, and she bucked back against me, wanting more of my dick even though there was no room.

Once she was finished, I let myself go—adding another load into her already full cunt. I lay on top of her as I filled her, dumping my seed inside her where it would remain until I fucked her again. I didn't moan the way I had last night, not when the sensation felt so raw. My eyes locked on to hers as I finished because I wanted her to understand how much I enjoyed her. I hadn't fucked around since I'd met her because I wasn't an idiot. I knew she had the best pussy I'd find anywhere.

I slowly pulled out and admired the white come dripping from her entrance. The sight was enough to turn me on all over again. Lucian was at home plotting his revenge against me, knowing full well I was coming inside his wife —over and over.

Soon enough, she would have so much come inside her that he wouldn't even want her back.

I got off her then pulled on my boxers.

She laid her head back down and closed her eyes, like she was ready to go back to sleep.

I stared at her beautiful body on the bed, the endless curves and the sexy olive skin. She was the only woman who held my attention even after I came. Everyone else was forgotten the second the fun was over. "You want some lunch?"

"Only if you're making French toast."

"That's not lunch. That's breakfast."

"Whatever."

"And no...I don't eat French toast."

"Do you ever have a cheat meal?" she asked incredulously. "What's the point in working so hard if you don't enjoy yourself once in a while."

"I do enjoy myself—with pussy."

She sat up and finally got out of bed. "That's not the only reason women want to sleep with you."

"Then why else?" I knew this woman was insanely attracted to me. I could see it in her eyes, the way she gripped my ass and pulled me deeper inside her.

She pulled out a shirt from one of my drawers. "I'm not going to inflate your already big ego." She walked into the kitchen, in just my t-shirt and a new thong from the pile she'd started to keep in my dresser.

I followed behind her, mesmerized by the sexy way her hips shook back and forth. I entered the kitchen and watched her make a bowl of cereal while I prepared my usual salmon. "My ego is already pretty big, so I don't think you can make it bigger."

She leaned against the counter and ate while I cooked at the stove. "Forget it. I'm not telling you."

"Ever?"

"Ever." Her teeth crunched against the cereal in her mouth.

"Seems unfair. I admit all the things I like about you." I flipped the salmon over and grilled the other side while the veggies sautéed in the other pan.

She kept eating, her hair a mess because I'd wrapped it around my hand so tightly. "You've admitted no such thing."

"I disagree."

"Then what?" she asked. "What do you find so fuckable about me?"

"I'll answer you—if you answer me." The fish only took a few minutes for each side, so I was done quickly. I slid the food onto a plate and abandoned the dirty pans on the stove. I glanced at her before I carried my food to the kitchen table.

She followed me, bringing her cereal with her. "Fine. You go first." She sat in the chair across from me with her bowl in front of her. She left the spoon in the milk and let the pieces of cereal grow soggy.

"Alright." I took a bite and swallowed. "I wanted to fuck you the moment I saw you because of your confidence. You sucked that olive into your mouth without the least bit of shame, hinting at all the sexy things you could do to my dick. Instead of coming over to me, you successfully called me over to you. That's impressive because I'm not much of a chaser. I couldn't turn down that olive skin, those firm tits that pushed against your dress. You were playful, mysterious. You're the most desirable woman in the world. Why else would Lucian make you his wife? He didn't have to take a spouse. He could have just had you as another mistress. You were too valuable of a prize not to claim. Now when I fuck you, I feel like I'm screwing a very talented virgin, someone so enthused it's like their first time. You pull me up against the car and ask me to fuck you underneath the night sky even though I already made you come several times. You're voracious, insatiable. You're the kind of woman that makes me feel like a man."

She listened to every word without a reaction, probably unsure how to respond to such blunt compliments. She looked down at her cereal and stirred the remaining pieces without taking a bite. After she cleared her throat, she lifted her gaze to look at me. "Women don't just want to fuck you because of your eight-pack and rock-hard chest. You're confident, intense, and mysterious. You get this look in your eyes that's just so possessive... It makes me feel naked even when I'm fully clothed. You're strong, so it makes me feel safe, like nothing could ever hurt me. Lucian is a powerful man, despite what you think. He's executed dozens of men right before my eyes. He has incredible allies. I've never seen anyone disrespect him and terrify him the way you do."

I noticed she didn't mention my wealth. A lot of women wished they could be the woman on my arm so they could be decorated in jewels and expensive things. They wanted my money as well as my power. That didn't seem important to this woman. All she really cared about was being protected.

Probably because she hadn't felt safe in so long.

The man she trusted betrayed her and let her become a prisoner. She wasn't gone long before he moved on and married someone else. Then a cruel man made her life unbearable every single day. Now she had a new owner. More than anything else in the world, she just wanted to feel safe.

There was no safer place in the world than by my side.

I cut into my salmon and kept eating.

She stirred her cereal and looked down into her milk. Now the bits were too soggy to be eaten, but she continued to play with them.

"So, you hate me?" I had been sheathed to the hilt when she'd said those words to me. She despised me, but she still wanted me.

"Yes." She got tired of playing with her food and pushed her bowl away.

"You hate me but want me all to yourself?"

"Hatred and lust aren't mutually exclusive."

"But they don't go hand in hand either." I kept eating. "And why do you hate me so much?" I didn't raise a hand to her or force her to do something she didn't want to do. Even when she threw a tantrum, I put food outside her door so she wouldn't starve. Her living arrangements could be much worse.

"It's pretty clear."

"Not to me."

Her green eyes flashed in hostility, her rage palpable with just a look. "I'm locked up in a tower with no rights. I have a tracker in my ankle, and I'm not allowed to leave. If you're as much of a man as you seem to be, you wouldn't need to keep me locked away. As a free woman, I would keep bedding you because I like it. Only a shadow of a man coerces a woman."

"I've never coerced you."

"I woke up last night, and you were inside me—"

"Because you were saying my name with your fingers inside your panties. We both know you wanted it, so let's not pretend."

She still wore that angry expression but didn't argue with me.

"And we both know I did you a favor. You prefer me to him—a million times over."

"That was before you captured me."

"You want me to give you back, then?" I challenged. "Because I will."

She didn't call my bluff. Going back to Lucian was far too appalling for her to gamble. "I thought you were rescuing me."

"I did rescue you."

"Then why don't I have any rights?"

"I told you if you wanted freedom you had to earn it." And she'd started to earn it last night when she confessed she didn't want to share me with anyone. She pulled me deep inside her and revealed her possessiveness. Maybe she did hate me, but she was also obsessed with me. My bed was the only one she wanted to sleep in every night.

"And what was last night?"

"A good start."

She sighed with irritation, her eyes showing her frustration. "What kind of freedoms can I earn?"

She could have whatever she wanted if she played her cards right. "A special team will escort you wherever you want to go at any time. You'll have my cash so you can buy anything you want. If you want to visit your family, you can. If you want to go out with friends, you can. But you will always sleep here with me. It's the safest place for you."

She probably wanted her own apartment for independence, but she didn't argue with me when I offered most of the things she wanted. "And when will that start?"

"When you've earned it."

"I need a time frame. My brothers haven't heard from me in a long time, and they'll get worried."

"I gave you a phone."

"I can't remember their numbers. Who memorizes phone numbers anymore?"

"Then they'll have to worry about you a little longer."

She turned angry, like she wanted to throw the bowl at my head again. "This is a two-way street. You want me to work for the things I want, but you need to give me the things I need. My family is everything to me, and I can't make them suffer like this. You will take me to them so I can explain what's going on."

No one else would attempt to make demands when it came to me. They would just accept what was offered out of fear of being stabbed in the throat. But this petite woman fought for the things she wanted and held her own in an argument. It was impressive. "I'll consider your request."

"No, you will—"

"I said I would consider it." My plate was empty, so I rose to my feet and carried it into the kitchen. I took her bowl too since it was obvious she was done with it. I enjoyed watching her make her demands, but I had to keep the authority in the situation. She had to understand she couldn't get what she wanted simply by issuing commandments. I responded to action, not words.

9

CASSINI

Instead of arguing with my captor, I needed to accept my situation. Balto wasn't as cruel as Lucian and respected me to a certain degree, but he wasn't a pushover. He had all the control in the situation, and he refused to accommodate me. Unless his demands were met, he would hold out forever.

I had to give in.

I had to be whatever he wanted me to be, to be so valuable that he would never want to give me up. He wanted me to be his lover, the woman who satisfied all of his needs. Once I upheld my end of the bargain, I'd finally reclaim some freedom.

It was bullshit, but that didn't matter.

Life wasn't fair—and it certainly wasn't fair to me.

My tantrum lasted the entire day and past dinner. I stayed in my room and tried to subdue my stubborn attitude. I examined this situation from every single angle, and there was no escape. There was no possibility of me ever walking free. Even if I could, Lucian would hunt me down, and I'd be back to square one.

Balto was right about one thing—he was the only one who could protect me.

Making the best of this situation was the only option I had.

I went into the dining room and found him at the table. He'd just finished a plate of grilled chicken with a side of broccoli. He skipped the carbs for every single meal, and it was so extreme that it was nauseating.

I couldn't eat like that if I tried. My family owned a pasta company, so forsaking carbs simply wasn't possible. My mother had made pasta at least three nights a week. It was how I grew up.

Balto relaxed in his chair as he looked at me. "I have extra if you want any."

"No thanks."

He rose from his chair, set his dishes in the sink, and then headed to his bedroom. He wasn't bothered by my coldness. He seemed completely indifferent to it.

"Are you leaving tonight?" I dreaded the nights when I was left alone. I didn't have a choice but to sleep on the couch and wait for him to return. There was a powerful man hunting me. Lucian wouldn't give up so easily. He might be afraid of Balto, but he was extremely intelligent. He wouldn't let me go without a fight.

He stopped and turned around, wearing nothing but his black sweatpants. The muscles of his back were always so tight, so thick with strength. Even the slightest movement caused a rippling effect. "No."

I couldn't hide my relief. When I'd slept in his bed last

night, it had been the greatest evening of sleep I'd ever gotten. There were no depressing dreams or nightmares. I didn't have a care in the world because this behemoth of a man was beside me.

He stared at me like he expected me to say something else. When I didn't, he turned around and walked off. His footsteps receded into his bedroom then he shut the door.

I stayed put and stared down the hallway. I'd ignored him all day, and then when I was ready to look at his face, he disappeared. Maybe he was avoiding me on purpose, or maybe he wasn't going to let my presence dictate what he would do next. It was only eight o' clock, so I doubted he was going to sleep.

I returned to my bedroom and looked through the clothes in my drawers. There was an assortment of lingerie he'd gotten me. All black and slutty—he had very specific tastes. He never asked me to wear them, but the fact that he bought them indicated that was what he wanted. I picked a one-piece that pushed my tits together with a crotch that unfastened and looked at myself in the mirror.

I looked like I belonged in a strip club.

I walked to his bedroom and heard the sound of gunshots firing off, like he was watching a movie or playing a video game. I opened the door without knocking and found him leaning back against the headboard, a gaming controller in his hands. His eyes were focused on the TV.

I was surprised this powerful man had such an amateur hobby.

I approached the bed and finally got his attention.

He glanced at me then turned back to the TV. It seemed to take him a second to register what I was wearing. He turned back instantly, admiring the black sequins that hugged my hourglass frame.

He set the controller to the side and didn't take his eyes off me. Gunshots continued until his character was killed and the Game Over screen appeared. That intense expression entered his gaze, his blue eyes so scorching they burned. The muscles of his chest and stomach tightened noticeably as he took in my appearance.

I never put on lingerie willingly, and I loved the way he stared at me. Putting on sex clothes would normally make me self-conscious, but when he looked at me like that, I felt like the sexiest thing in the world.

He kept his eyes on me as he grabbed the top of his sweats and pushed them down to his thighs, letting his hard cock stretch out and lie against his stomach. The crown was thick and tinted red with blood because he'd ballooned up to size in less than a minute. "Come here, baby."

I crawled on the bed and straddled his hips.

His hands immediately gripped my waist, and his fingers dug into my skin. He squeezed me as he pulled me down so I could feel his hardness right against my clit. He rested against the headboard as his eyes admired the thin material that barely hid my naked body from view. He appreciated the sight like I was a fantasy, like he'd never seen anything more beautiful. His fingers slid to the apex of my thighs, and he unfastened the clasp that kept the material over my cunt. Once it was open, he pressed his fingers against my clit and rubbed me gently.

I closed my eyes when I felt his intimate touch. Pleasure radiated all through my body because he touched the sensitive area just right. He applied the perfect kind of pressure without hitting me too hard. It felt the same as when I touched myself.

He pulled his fingers away then gripped my hips. He started to move my body, making me drag my clit against his throbbing length. He guided me back and forth as he rocked back into me, using his dick to apply the same pressure.

My hands snaked up his chest, and I forgot that I'd come in here to orchestrate my demands. I'd intended to seduce him so I could see my brothers tomorrow, but now I was the one being seduced. My breathing turned labored, and my nails clawed at his skin. My palms snaked up to his shoulders so I could use his frame as an anchor in order to rock my hips harder. My clit dragged against his length, and I felt the climax approach.

"You look so fucking sexy right now." He stared at my tits as he clenched his jaw. "The second my cock is buried in that pussy, I'm gonna come. So I need you to come now." He maneuvered me harder, making me feel the friction even deeper.

Hearing the longing in his deep voice and seeing the desire in his gorgeous eyes sent me over the edge. I leaned into him and pressed my forehead to his as I dragged my clit against him harder. The orgasm hit me deep inside even though he wasn't buried between my legs. Like all the other climaxes he gave me, I combusted like an inferno, burning everything around me. Against my will, I whispered his name, said it so many times I couldn't keep track.

His hand fisted my hair, and he kissed me hard, kissed me like my performance turned him on so deeply. He claimed me as his own, made me feel like his woman, not his prisoner. His hand slid between my legs, and he slipped two fingers inside my cunt. When he felt the wetness lubricate his fingertips, he moaned into my mouth. "Get on my dick. Now." He released my hair and pulled his fingers out of my cunt. Then he grabbed his length and pointed his head at my entrance.

I was lost in a trance, but I had to focus on my goal. I had to focus on the reason I'd come in here in the first place. "I want to see my family tomorrow." I rose on my knees so he couldn't force his way between my lips.

He wore the exact same expression, as if he didn't hear a word I said. "They say you should never provoke a hungry bear. That's when they're the most violent, the most unpredictable."

I recognized the threat in his tone.

"Now fuck me." He grabbed my hips and dragged me down.

I fought against him. "Take me to see my family tomorrow, and I will."

The anger entered his gaze, and his jaw tightened so deeply it seemed like it might snap. "I'll think about it."

"No. I want your word."

His nostrils flared as he stared me down.

"You aren't going to fuck me until I get what I want."

"And you're going to regret doing this to me." His hand moved to my neck, and he squeezed me gently. "I will punish you."

I could deal with the punishment later, but I needed to see my brothers now. "I don't care."

His eyes shifted back and forth as he looked into mine.

His cock was still rock-hard underneath me, like my disobedience turned him on even more. "Alright. I will take you to see your family tomorrow."

I'd finally secured what I wanted, a bit of freedom to tell my brothers what happened to me. They were probably worried sick. They probably even called Lucian to figure out what happened. There was nothing my brothers wouldn't do for me, even speak to that asshole.

"And you will pay for this little stunt." He yanked me hard down his length, forcing himself inside without giving me the gentleness I was used to. He pulled me down all the way so his entire length could sit inside me, surrounded by my wetness and tightness. He inhaled a deep breath as he enjoyed it, his cock twitching noticeably inside me. "Fuck me. Hard." He guided my hips up and down, showing me the pace he wanted.

I finally secured what I wanted, even though I would pay for it later, so I upheld my end of the bargain. I gripped his shoulders and bounced up and down, taking his length all the way to his balls. He was impressively long, so I had to rise high before I slid back down to sheathe his entire length.

Once Balto got what he wanted, he rested his hands on my thighs and watched me fuck him. He watched my tits shake and my thighs tighten as I slid up and down, taking in every single inch the way he liked. "You're going to be so sore tomorrow, baby. I promise you."

H e made good on his word.

I woke up the next morning feeling the pain between my legs. He took me all night long, and even when I fell asleep, he climbed on top of me and fucked me anyway. My small size couldn't take his huge cock for more than a few hours, and now I was paying the price for having something so large inside me, fucking me so hard indefinitely.

I opened my eyes and looked beside me, seeing that Balto was dead asleep. His muscular chest rose and fell slowly with his deep breaths, and it was surprising how much he resembled a bear in hibernation. He was massive, intimidating, and still terrifying even when he was asleep.

Despite the pain I experienced, I'd still slept well.

It was nice having him in the building through the night.

I knew Balto would keep his word and take me to see my brothers, so I got in the shower and got ready for the day. The weather was cooling now that we were in the middle of autumn, so I wore jeans and a long-sleeved shirt with a v neck. Balto didn't just buy me slutty clothes that made me look like a whore. He also had purchased jeans and t-shirts, casual stuff I could wear while getting a cup of coffee. Lucian was different. He wanted me dressed like a beauty queen at all times.

I made a bowl of cereal when Balto came down the hallway. In his black sweatpants with slightly messy hair, he poured himself a cup of coffee then opened the fridge.

I stared at his muscular back and thought about the night before. He'd made me sit in his lap the entire time, riding his dick over and over until he couldn't come anymore. He used me like a toy rather than a human. It didn't feel like a punishment at all until the soreness kicked in. I wondered if that was the punishment, or if he had something else in mind.

He pulled out a container of egg whites along with veggies. "I know I should stop asking, but do you want any?"

"Never."

"Alright. I'll stop asking." He poured the egg whites into the pan and prepared his breakfast.

There was a bowl of fruit on the counter, so I grabbed a banana and ate that standing up. "When are we going to leave?"

"After I finish my workout."

"How long is your workout?"

"An hour and a half."

I couldn't even watch TV that long, let alone exercise that long.

"Where do they live?"

"They're both at work during the day."

"Then should we wait until they're home?"

"No. They work together, so that's the best way to see them at the same time."

He scooped his food onto a plate and grabbed a fork. Instead of carrying his food to the kitchen table, he stood at the counter and ate. "What do they do?" He scooped a bite into his mouth and chewed. Despite how pissed he was last night, he didn't seem angry anymore.

"They run a pasta company. It belonged to my grand-parents, and it was passed to my parents. Now it belongs to the three of us."

He stopped chewing mid-bite. His eyes slowly turned to me before he started to chew again. When he finished, he set his plate on the counter beside him even though he hadn't finished his food. "What pasta company is this?"

"Cardello Italian Cuisine."

He stared at me blankly, like that name actually meant something to him.

"What?"

His silence continued as he crossed his arms over his chest.

"I doubt you recognize the name since you never eat carbs."

"That's your maiden name? Cardello?"

"Yes."

He looked straight ahead across the kitchen. Then he departed, leaving behind his food and abruptly dismissing the conversation.

Did he know my brothers? I didn't see how that could be possible. My brothers did respectable work, while Balto was a criminal. But maybe he knew all the business owners in this city since it was his territory. I followed behind him until I entered his bedroom. "Do you know them or something?"

He pulled out his workout clothes from the dresser and changed. He slipped on his workout shoes without addressing my question. Then he grabbed his earbuds and walked past me.

"Are you going to answer me?" I demanded, annoyed by his silence.

"I'll be back in an hour and a half." He kept walking, dismissing me.

I had no idea what his coldness meant, but I would figure it out at some point today.

WE LEFT in his truck and headed across the city to where the factory was located. Not once did Balto ask where the business was located. He made all the right turns like he knew exactly where he was going.

He pulled up to the front of the building and parked along the curb.

"I should go in alone."

He killed the engine and stared straight ahead. "I'll give you fifteen minutes."

"This is going to take longer than fifteen minutes."

"Fifteen minutes until I join you."

"I really don't think that's a good idea…" My brothers never tolerated Lucian, and they definitely wouldn't tolerate Balto. Case would be particularly vicious. Balto wasn't afraid of anything, so he might actually hurt one of my brothers if there was too much back talk.

"I disagree."

If I'd known that, I wouldn't have tried to see my brothers in the first place. "You can't lay a hand on them. I mean it."

"I can lay a hand on anyone I want."

"I mean it, Balto." I stared at him until he met my gaze.

He stared at me with his pretty blue eyes. As a little boy, he must have been so adorable. But now that he was a man, those beautiful, soft eyes didn't show even a hint of innocence. "In my world, no one is immune. If they cross me, I'll have no choice. My best advice to you is to make sure that doesn't happen."

"I can't control them—"

"And you can't control me." He faced forward again. "Fifteen minutes."

I'd made my bed, so now I had to lie in it. I left the truck and walked inside the building. After moving down the hallways, I reached the kitchen where Case and Dirk experimented with different recipes. Neither one of them was there, so I continued farther back to the table where Case did all the paperwork. Case sat there, a bottle of scotch sitting next to an empty glass. Dark circles were under his eyes, and it seemed like he hadn't slept in days.

I knew the reason why. "Case?"

Case's head snapped in my direction quickly, his reflexes sharp. His eyes took me in with shock followed by relief. "Cassini?" He jumped out of his chair and came toward me. "Jesus Christ, where the hell have you been? I've been calling all week, and your phone is off. I tried to get a hold of Lucian, but he didn't answer." He reached me and wrapped his arms around me, holding me in a way that almost never happened. The last time he'd hugged me like this was when our father passed away.

"Case, I'm alright."

He held me for a moment before he released me. "If you're alright, then what the hell is going on? You usually check in every few days, and then you just disappear. Did that bastard do something to you?"

"No, this is what happened—"

"I've gotta call Dirk." He snatched his phone off the table and made the call. "Cassini just showed up." He stood with his hand on his hip, still looking pissed even though I was in one piece. "Yeah, she's fine. Get your ass up here." He hung up and tossed the phone back onto the table. "We were prepared to ambush him if it came down to it."

"That doesn't surprise me." When I told him what really happened, he'd want to ambush someone else.

Dirk ran in a second later, relief on his face at the sight of me. But once he realized I was safe and in one piece, he turned back to the cold and indifferent younger brother. "Don't pull that stunt again, alright? Case and I were losing our minds." He came up to me and gave me a one-armed hug.

"I'll try."

Dirk stood beside Case, his arms crossed over his chest. "What happened? Did he take your phone away or something?"

"He's never done anything like that before." Case was dressed in a gray t-shirt and jeans, tiny drops of sauce splattered across his clothes because he must have been in the kitchen earlier. He had muscular arms and narrow hips, his body type similar to Balto's.

"It's a long story," I began. "And you aren't going to like it…"

Case's visage darkened noticeably.

Dirk inhaled a deep breath in preparation.

"Lucian has one enemy that he's actually afraid of. I've never seen him sweat like a pig, never seen him turn so lifeless. But when this guy walks into a room…he practically cowers." Lucian was the definition of weak. He punched me in the stomach because I was easy to overpower, but when it came to a real opponent, he turned into the world's biggest pussy. He let Balto burn his hand without even trying to stop him—because he knew it was a fight he couldn't possibly win. "We were at the opera house when this man showed up and burned a cigar into his hand. Killed Lucian's men without making a single noise. I guess Lucian stole from him and didn't fulfill his end of the deal."

"What's the point in all this?" Case asked. "Is this relevant?"

"Very." I knew I only had minutes left before Balto stormed into the place and caused trouble. "The man came back to the house one night and told Lucian to give back what he stole. Or offer his complete allegiance. When Lucian didn't cooperate…he took me."

Case didn't react right away because the knowledge was too much to absorb.

Dirk's eyebrows practically popped off his forehead.

"I've been living with him ever since," I continued. "He didn't give me a phone or freedom until now. There's a tracker in my ankle, so I can't run away. And this guy…

makes Lucian look like a child. Before you start throwing out threats—"

"Who the fuck is this guy?" Case snapped. "I'll stab him in the neck with just a pen and watch him bleed out and die. Who the fuck does he think he is? You're a person, for fuck's sake. Not a prized horse that can change hands for the right price."

I hated being treated that way too. I hadn't been a free woman in a long time. I was a piece of property people fought over. They wanted my beauty and the prize between my legs.

"Who is he?" Dirk asked.

"There's nothing you can do, so please don't start anything." Balto wouldn't hesitate to hurt my brothers if they became difficult. I had to keep them calm before Balto marched inside. "He told me he would kill both of you if you moved against him."

"I'd like to see him try." Case's nostrils flared.

"He's going to walk in here in a few minutes," I said. "He's sitting outside in the truck."

"Is he doing this to torture us?" Case asked. "To dangle his prize in front of our faces?"

"No...we're here because I asked him to bring me." I didn't want them to worry about me. I wanted them to know I was safe. "He's a cruel man, but if I'm being honest...I prefer him to Lucian. What I want most is my freedom, to be my own person again. But that's clearly never going to happen...so at least he's better than Lucian."

Case's nostrils flared again. "Who is he, Cassini?"

"I'm sure you don't know him," I said. "He's the leader of some criminal cult. He's gone most nights doing god knows what. If he scares Lucian, then he really must be dangerous. When he walks in here, maybe it's best if you say nothing—"

"Who the fuck is he?" Case stepped forward, his eyes shifting back and forth with hostility.

My brothers were honest men who ran their pasta company. They worked long hours and made a quality product that had been in our family for generations. Even when the price of goods rose, they did their best to keep their product at the same price for customers. They made a handsome living from the enterprise, but at the cost of their blood, sweat, and tears. Honest men like them would have no idea who my captor was. They wouldn't understand the true ramifications of the situation. "His name is Balto. I don't know his last name."

Case's entire body slackened noticeably, like that name meant something to him.

Dirk stepped forward too. "Balto...as in the Skull King?"

I'd never heard that title before. "The Skull what?"

"Skull King." Case had his arms crossed over his chest, but he dropped them at the revelation. "That Balto?"

I raised an eyebrow. "You know him?"

Case nodded. "Unfortunately. Does he wear a ring on his right hand, an image of a skull carved out of a flawless diamond?"

Shit, they did know him. "Yes..."

Dirk pressed his palms against his face and dragged them down to his chin. "Shit."

Case kept staring at me, his jaw clenched tight and his eyes unblinking. He sighed as he closed his eyes for a long pause.

"How do you know him?" I was married to a criminal, and I hadn't heard of Balto until recently. How did these two pasta makers know the biggest criminal in this city?

Case never gave me an answer. "How long has this been going on?"

"I've stayed with him for almost three weeks." Now I was in his bed a lot more often than my own. I used sex as a weapon, but I suspected I would regret that soon enough.

"You said he's better than Lucian," Case said. "That means he treats you better?" Case couldn't keep the pain out of his eyes, the fact that he couldn't protect me from the horrors in this world.

"Yes, he does." I couldn't look into his eyes because the pain was too much. "He's never laid a hand on me. He's never forced me to do anything I didn't want to do. He lets me eat whatever I want. I don't have any freedom yet, but he said he'll give it to me when I earn it."

Case didn't ask how I would earn that freedom. He wasn't clueless as to my value to men. He knew exactly what they wanted me for. But it was too disturbing to say out loud.

"I know Lucian will do whatever he can to get me back, but I don't think he stands a chance against Balto." I would be safe as long as Balto wanted me to be safe.

"No, he doesn't," Case admitted quietly.

A moment later, heavy footsteps sounded behind me. The impact of his large size was audible with every step he took. My back was to him, but I could feel his power radiate across my back as if I were standing next to a roaring fire.

Case looked up and stared at him, his vulnerability dying away as he turned into the cold and hard man he projected himself to be. It was the image he showed to strangers and enemies, not family.

Dirk did the same, staring him down like his number one enemy.

Balto slowly came to my side but didn't touch me. He stared down my brother with the same ferocity, silently warning him that it would be unwise to draw a weapon. He was the same height as Case, over half a foot taller than me. His casual attire didn't make him any less formidable. He could be completely naked, and he would be the most intimidating man on the planet. "Case."

Case stared him down. "Asshole."

I closed my eyes at the insult, praying this bad situation didn't get worse.

"Asshole?" Balto asked, his voice full of amusement. "I saved your sister from a spineless psychopath."

"Then save her from yourself—and let her go." Case addressed Balto like I wasn't even there. They were two enemies on opposite sides of the battlefield. "My sister isn't some show animal. She's a fucking Cardello, and you will release her." Case was either very dumb or very brave, because he stepped closer to Balto and got in his face.

Balto didn't retreat an inch. "What happens when Lucian hunts her down? We both know you won't do a damn thing. If you could, you would have rescued her in the first place. But you did nothing. Not a fucking thing." Balto took a step forward, forcing Case back. "I took her. So she's mine."

"She'll never be yours, asshole," Case spat. "A man can't own a woman who doesn't want to be owned. A real man can get a woman without paying her or stealing her. The

fact that you have to force her just shows who you really are
—a pathetic jackass."

Balto could have mentioned our affair and the fact that
it was completely consensual. I was the one calling him
most of the time. I was the one who never wanted to leave
his arms. But he kept that information private.

"Let her go." Case did something really stupid and
shoved Balto in the chest.

Like a mountain, Balto didn't move. He only looked
amused. "Be careful, Case. Your sister asked me not to hurt
you, but if you touch me again, I'll have to break your
hand."

Just as I anticipated, Case pulled his fist back to punch
him in the face.

I grabbed his elbow and pushed him back. "Case, stop.
It's not going to change anything."

Case pushed me off, handling me with more aggression
than he ever had before. "She's been through enough. Let
her go."

Balto looked just as amused as he did at the beginning
of the conversation. "Never."

The hope left my lungs with the breath I took. I didn't
know how long I would be a prisoner to this man, but
forever was such a burden, I could barely take it.

"Lucian crossed me—and she's the key to torturing
him." Balto stepped forward. "I took one of his most valuable possessions, and it's driving him mad this very instant.
He'll either give me what I want in exchange for her, or
he'll make a move against me—and lose. Your sister is the
key to all of this. So don't expect to ever get her back."

Hearing the finality in his voice made me realize there

was no hope. I could either be valuable to Balto long enough that by the time he lost interest in me, Lucian wouldn't want me. Or I could be handed back to Lucian in exchange for precious commodities. Both options weren't great, but I had the best opportunity for freedom with Balto. Or maybe I would get lucky and someone else would kill Lucian. With him out of the way, I could cut out the tracker in my ankle and run away. This wasn't how I wanted to spend my twenties, but accepting my situation was less painful than fighting against it. Balto was too powerful to overcome. He was the most ruthless man in this country. I didn't stand a chance, and neither did my brothers.

Case stood there, speechless. There was so much rage on his face, but there was nothing he could do with it. His hands balled into fists as he stood there, completely helpless.

Dirk stared down Balto like he was considering stabbing him in the gut.

"Case." I gripped his arm and dragged him away along with Dirk. "You need to let this go."

"How do you expect me to do that?" he hissed, his voice quiet. "I'm just supposed to be okay with this? You have no idea who that man is. He's a psychotic murderer. There's no line that man won't cross. Maybe you prefer him to Lucian now, but when you really get to know him, you won't feel that way."

Maybe that was true, but this was the hand I'd been dealt. "Eventually, he'll get tired of me. Hopefully that happens when Lucian is dead or has moved on. Then there's no reason why he won't let me go."

"Or he'll kill you." Case glanced at him over my shoulder.

Maybe I didn't know the man like I thought I did, but I couldn't picture him killing me without reason. There had been lots of times when I disobeyed him and tested his temper, but not once did he punch me in the stomach. I told him off to his face, and there were never repercussions. He said he would punish me for my stunt last night, but if he were going to hurt me, he would have done it already. "I don't think he'll do that."

"Then you don't know him very well," Dirk said. "You have no idea who this man really is. He's the Skull King. He runs this country in plain sight. He owns the police, the prisons, and all the criminals. This guy has his thumb pressed into everyone."

With a title like that, I didn't doubt he was a scary man. But I wasn't a criminal or an enemy. I was just a woman. "I'm just trying to be optimistic."

"That might help you sleep at night," Case said. "But that doesn't help us. You deserve to be free. Deserve to be happy."

"Well...I've learned that life isn't fair." I looked my brother in the eye. "We play with the hand we're dealt and hope we get a better card. I'm in this situation because of a bad decision...and now I have to face the consequences."

"Yes, you should learn your lesson," Case said. "But you shouldn't be punished forever. We'll find a way to get you out, Cassini. I promise."

I squeezed his arm. "The last thing I want is for something to happen to you. There's nothing we can do against this man. Getting yourselves killed will only hurt me more.

The best thing we can do is remain calm...and hope for the best."

Balto grew impatient with our private conversation. "Baby, let's go."

I was surprised he'd called me that in public. It seemed like something he only did in private, unless he was trying to get a rise out of my brothers. "I'll see you soon." I hugged both of them. "I love you both."

"We love you too." Case released me reluctantly, like it was the hardest thing he'd ever had to do.

"I'll be okay." It wasn't a lie, but it wasn't the truth either. I just wanted to say something to ease his worry, to make this less unbearable. "I'll see you soon." I walked back to Balto, who wore the same icy expression.

Dressed in all black with short hair, he looked like the formidable man my brothers described him as. Even without that ring on his hand, he seemed like the criminal warlord he was rumored to be. I hadn't been a victim of his cruelty, but I believed he was capable of terrible things.

I came to his side with a pained expression. I was relieved I got to see my brothers, but I wasn't happy with the air of sadness I was leaving behind. They wanted to protect me because it was their job now that Father was gone—but it wasn't possible.

Balto looked at me with the same hard expression, unaffected by the emotion in my eyes. The man was cold as ice and dry like a sponge. He couldn't absorb the feelings around him because he was incapable of it. His eyes bored into mine a moment longer before he turned away. "The only reason Case is alive is because of you."

11

BALTO

I could have put Case and Dirk on the spot by mentioning their drug operation in the factory, but since I wasn't a rat, I didn't throw them under the bus. It was obvious Cassini had no idea what her brothers were up to, but they could share that information with her.

It wasn't my place.

And I didn't mention the fact that Cassini and I were having an affair for about a month before I took her. Our secret relationship was heated, passionate, and so scorching that I lost all interest in other women. I could have said their sister liked having me between her legs.

But again, I wasn't a rat.

So I kept all their secrets to myself. I seemed to know more about their family than they did.

We drove back to the building, and I parked the truck.

"You need to give me more freedom." She made the demand like she somehow had the right.

Her attitude always amused me. "I don't have to do

anything." I got out of the truck and walked inside the elevator.

She came with me. "I could stay with Case during the nights you're gone. I hate being here alone."

We rose to the top floor and stepped inside the living room. "You aren't alone."

"But you aren't here, so there's no reason for me to be here."

I turned to look at her. "I want you here when I get home."

"Then I'll come back before you—"

"I don't need another man to look after my woman. Just because I'm not here doesn't mean I'm not protecting you. Just because I'm not physically here doesn't mean I'm not watching you. The answer is no. It'll always be no." I ignored the disappointed look on her face and walked into the kitchen to make lunch. I poured a glass of scotch and enjoyed that while I worked the pans.

She sat at the dining table, her chin propped on her knuckles and her eyes filled with a haze. Her thoughts were far away, thinking about her interaction with her brothers.

I finished making my lunch then took the seat across from her. "You aren't going to eat anything?"

"Not hungry."

I stared at her thick, pouted lips as I ate, sipping my scotch every now and then.

"So, how are you going to punish me?"

"You'll see."

"Are you going to hurt me?" She lowered both hands to the table and stared at her fingers, unable to meet my gaze as she waited to hear my answer.

I didn't have a problem striking anyone who crossed me, even if it was a woman, but I had no urge to lay a hand on her. The last thing I wanted to do was hurt her, to bruise her beautiful skin and make her wince in pain. I enjoyed hurting my enemies, but that was because they deserved it. "No."

She lifted her gaze to meet mine. "Will you ever hurt me?"

I didn't want to be honest because she would assume she could get away with anything. But I didn't need violence to keep her in line. There were a million other things I could do. "No."

Her eyes softened slightly.

"Violence isn't the only way to keep someone in line."

"Punishing me and keeping me in line are two very different things. I don't think you'll ever be able to keep me in line."

"I'm up for the challenge." I ate everything on my plate then enjoyed my scotch as I looked at her.

"Isn't it a little early to be drinking?"

"It's never too early." My schedule was all over the place. Sometimes I went to bed early, sometimes I didn't sleep at all. Time didn't mean the same thing to me as it did to everyone else. "Want some?" I pushed the glass across the surface toward her.

She pushed it back. "I'm not a scotch kinda lady."

My hand slid it across the table toward her. "That's gonna have to change."

"Why?" She left the glass in front of her.

"You're gonna have a hard time fitting in at the Underground."

"What's the Underground?"

"Our headquarters. You were near there for a brief time when I took you from Lucian." Or at least, she was in the parking lot of an adjacent building.

She finally took a drink and didn't make a face when it moved down her throat. "I still don't see what the fuss is about. And if I drank as much as you, I'd be drunk all the time."

"I'd love to see you drunk."

"It's not very entertaining. I'm usually pretty quiet."

"Then I'll get you *really* drunk."

"What are you like drunk?"

I was always drunk. "How I am right now."

She raised an eyebrow.

"I haven't been sober in at least a decade."

"That's not good for your liver."

"I'm gonna die young anyway, so it doesn't matter."

"Why is that?" She set the glass in front of me.

"In my line of business, your career is short."

Now that we were talking, she wasn't in such a sour mood. She wore a white t-shirt that looked lovely against her skin tone. And her luscious hair moved past her chest, the strands dark and soft. "That doesn't bother you?"

"Not at all."

"Everyone is afraid to die."

"I'm more afraid of living too old. At a certain age, we become weak. I'd rather die at my strongest than be murdered at my weakest. I want to die with honor, not be hunted like a weak animal."

"Why would someone hunt you down? You would retire eventually then live a quiet life."

"Retirement isn't for everyone, especially me." I would sit alone in a large house and count down the days until death. Maybe my brother would still be around for company, but probably not. It would be a quiet and lonely existence, one without much purpose.

"You don't want to live peacefully with your wife and kids?"

I nearly did a double take because her question was so absurd. "Do I look like a family man to you? I pay for whores, and I've taken you prisoner for revenge. And you think I'll take a wife someday?"

She shrugged. "People change."

"Yes. But not drastically."

"Do you ever want that?"

I didn't bother answering her question. This was a stupid conversation.

When she didn't get an answer, she kept talking. "I know that's something I want. A husband, two kids, and a place outside the city with a yard."

She would never get it. She would either be my prisoner forever, return to Lucian, or die. There was no picture-perfect family in her future. I grabbed the glass and took a long drink. It'd been almost three weeks, and Lucian hadn't contacted me. I'd expected him to cave by now.

"So...they call you the Skull King?"

I lifted my right hand, showing the ring that distinguished my power. "Yes."

"And they call you that because of the ring?"

"No. I'm the Skull King because I'm in charge. The ring has nothing to do with it. It shows my fearlessness, that I wear this billion-euro ring constantly because I'm not scared that someone will try to steal it. In fact, I hope they do. Nothing I enjoy more than snapping an idiot's neck."

"Are you afraid someone will steal Lucian's?"

I shrugged. "I'm sure he hid it away somewhere safe now that he knows we're at war."

"What are the Skull Kings? What do you do, exactly?"

"The Skull Kings started decades ago as a group of assassins. If you paid the right price, the Skull Kings would kill anyone you wanted. Over time, it morphed into something else. Soon, they became arms dealers. Then it continued to expand more and more. Under my reign, we monitor everything in this country. I tax all of my criminals and take a percentage of their profits."

"Why would they agree to pay you?"

"Because they want to live," I said simply. "And protection. I keep the peace among the different factions, make sure no one is infringing on anyone else's territory. If someone is causing too many problems, I remove them."

"Does that mean Lucian pays you a tax?"

"No. Not everyone is under my reign. I have enemies like everyone else. They have their own alliance."

Cassini nodded slightly. "That's why you work all the time."

I nodded.

"And why you don't have a girlfriend."

"No. I don't have a girlfriend because having a girlfriend is pussy shit. I'm either fucking someone, or I'm not."

"So you're fucking me?"

I nodded.

"But you said I was your woman."

"Yes. You're the woman I'm fucking. It's that simple."

She would never mean anything to me, just as no woman ever meant anything to me.

"That sounds like a really bleak existence. All you do is work, and you don't have any real relationships. You don't love anyone, no one loves you. What's the point in risking your neck every night? You're already rich, so does more money really make a difference?"

"It's not just about the money."

"Then what's it about?"

"Power." I had the ability to do anything I wanted, to execute anyone without a single objection. I controlled this city, and that gave me purpose. Maybe I didn't have anything meaningful in my life, but I had that.

Cassini didn't seem impressed. "My happiest memories are the nights when my family would be gathered around the table, and we'd be drinking wine and eating bread. Mother would cook one of her delicious meals, and Father would drink way too much and tell stories he'd told a million times. It didn't matter how much money we had. Power was never relevant. Just being together made us the richest people in the world."

My parents died a long time ago, and the only family I had left was my obnoxious brother. We didn't have a happy childhood. We didn't have much of a childhood at all. "Not everyone can have a picture-perfect family."

"We weren't picture-perfect. That's the point."

The annoyance was beginning to get to me. She judged my lifestyle when she was dumb enough to open her legs for a man who didn't deserve her. "You aren't better than me, so stop acting like you are."

"I never said I was."

"You're acting like it. Turning up your nose at me like you've got it all figured out."

"Again, never said that. I'm just trying to understand you."

"I'm pretty simple—not much to understand."

"Yes...I've noticed." She turned quiet, detecting my rage. "When did you become the Skull King?"

"Five years ago."

"And how did that work? Did the man before you die?"

"No. He made a lot of bad decisions. The guys told him to step down, and he refused. So they elected me to defeat him by combat."

She raised an eyebrow. "What?"

"To replace an existing king, you must defeat him in battle. No weapons. Just fists."

"And you fight until someone gives up?" she asked incredulously.

"No. You fight to the death."

Her face immediately paled.

"Two kings can't live at the same time, not when the first refuses to step down. Causes too many problems."

"So, you killed him?" She was still in shock about the whole thing.

"Yes. I crushed his skull with my bare hands."

Now she didn't blink at all, as if she finally understood just how dangerous I was. "So, someone could challenge you?"

"Theoretically. But they won't."

"Why not?"

"Because I'm the best king we've ever had. My focus is on peace, not rivalry. I don't risk my men needlessly. I've also brought in more profits than the kings before me. Any time we're at war, I'm on the front lines. I don't hide in the back like previous leaders. I get my hands dirty. I expose myself to the flying bullets just like my soldiers. I don't send my men into battle unless I'm standing beside them."

She seemed overwhelmed, like she didn't understand the true extent of my profession. She looked down at the table, her eyes showing that her thoughts were a million miles away. Maybe understanding who I truly was would give her an incentive to behave.

But knowing her, she would disobey me anyway.

12

BALTO

"So when are we going to do this?" Heath asked.

We sat at the table with the two men I trusted most. Brutus was on my left, and Thomas was beside him. Brutus told me exactly where Hunter Reyes was doing business that week, so catching him off guard would be simple.

"We roll in with everything we got," Brutus said. "That should scare him shitless."

"I say we kill a few of his men just to send a message," Thomas said. "Preferably his kids."

"We aren't killing anyone until we know for certain." I sat in the high-backed chair with the skulls carved into the wood and my hand resting over the top of my glass. "We arrive and take a look at the scene. Depending on what we find, I'll make the decision then."

Heath was new to the position, but he caught on quickly. He was a smart man despite his dumb decisions, and the men didn't have a problem with him. "If he's really skimming that much cash, we gotta prove it. Because we can't let him get away with that shit."

One of my men walked inside. "Balto, I've got two men here to see you."

"I'm in a meeting. I'll speak with them afterward."

"They said it was urgent."

I lifted my gaze again to look at him. "Is that supposed to mean something to me? Who the hell are these guys?"

"Case and Dirk Cardello."

Cassini's brothers had arrived at my lair—to talk about Cassini, no doubt. I was surprised they came all the way down here on my territory. They were surrounded by my army, and if they stepped out of line for even a second, they were dead. They really were brave. "Send them in." I turned to Brutus. "Make all the arrangements. We'll hit them tomorrow night."

"Alright." Brutus and the guys left.

Heath lingered behind for a second. "If they think you're gonna change your mind, they're idiots."

I would never give up Cassini, no matter what kind of sob story they could tell. "Get out."

Heath flipped me off before he walked out.

A moment later, Case and Dirk entered. The door shut behind them, and two men guarded the door, both armed and ready to kill them if they made a move against me. Case wore a black leather jacket, and Dirk wore a long-sleeved olive shirt. They possessed the classic Italian features that Cassini also had. If all three of them appeared on a Christmas card, they would look like a beautiful family.

The topless bartender appeared and gave the guys two

glasses of scotch. She replaced my drink even though I was only halfway finished. Then she disappeared and gave us our privacy.

Case didn't touch his drink. His green eyes were full of irritation—all of which was directed at me.

Dirk was just as cold.

"You're wasting your time, boys." I shook the ice cubes before I took a drink. "I understand your grievance, but there's no way around it. Your sister is mine, and there's nothing you can do to get me to release her. I suggest you let it go." She might not have her freedom, but she was well taken care of.

"We have something to offer you." Case held on to his glass but didn't take a drink. "We negotiated fifteen percent of our business. Give up Cassini, and we'll give you fifty percent. You know what kind of numbers we're pulling. You know how much that leaves on the table. It's a generous offer."

It was a very generous offer, but Cassini was priceless. "No."

Case sighed loudly.

"Even if I agreed, you have no way to keep her safe from Lucian. He'd figure it out quickly enough, and you'd be powerless against him. Honestly, the safest place for her is right beside me."

"We'd figure something out," Case said. "We could sell the business and leave if it became necessary."

"That wouldn't work because I wouldn't be getting my cut."

Case shrugged. "We would find a way. We aren't going to give up on our sister."

Even though it was pointless, I admired his determination. "I rejected your offer, so you can leave." I'd taken Cassini from behind before I left, fucking her good and hard on my bed before I gave her a load to last her through the night.

"How about this?" Case asked. "Give her up...and we'll give you a hundred percent of the business."

That caught my attention because it was so desperate. "You'd be working for free."

"We're there for the pasta anyway. We would just keep whatever we needed to break even. The rest of it is yours. We're talking twenty million euro a month—for doing nothing." Case leaned forward and stared at me with enthusiasm, hoping that would tempt me into folding.

A small part of me felt guilty for keeping Cassini when her brothers wanted her freedom so much. It was obvious how much they loved her if they were willing to sacrifice everything for her. Those family dinners she mentioned must have been as wonderful as she remembered. It was a little heartbreaking to hear these men sacrifice everything for her. I had no one who would do anything like that for me. Heath was my brother, but I doubted he would walk away from that much money to save me. It was a huge sacrifice.

Case kept watching me. "We got a deal?"

It was tempting, but not tempting enough. "No."

Case slammed his fist onto the table. "Then what the hell do you want, Balto? Name it, and we'll give it to you."

Truth be told, there was nothing anyone could offer me that would tempt me. Cassini had captured my obsession from the moment I'd laid eyes on her. Without her in my bed, my sheets would be ice cold. Sex would be routine and stale. She set my world on fire and kept me warm. "There's nothing I want more than her."

Dirk shook his head. "Everything has a price."

"Not Cassini."

"We could do something to Lucian," Case offered. "Anything you want."

"Don't bother. Lucian is an opponent you can't match. For Cassini's sake, stay away from him. You won't come back alive."

"You underestimate us," Case said coldly.

"No," I said. "I'm just giving you a reality check. But I'll make a deal with you. I'll bring her by once a week so you can spend time with her. Once she and I work out our issues, she can come see you alone."

Case sighed, like that only annoyed him. "She's not an animal."

"And I don't treat her like she is. That woman is rich, protected, and safe. She can't run off and do whatever she wants yet, but she's treated like a queen." I gave that woman whatever she wanted, a life of luxury.

"Queens aren't captured and locked in a tower," Dirk snapped.

"That's the best I can offer you. Take it or leave it."

Case stared at his brother.

Dirk took a drink.

"What are you going to do with her?" Case asked. "When Lucian wants her back, you'll trade me for whatever he stole?"

I lifted my right hand. "He took one of my skull

diamonds. And I'm not sure if I'll trade her or not. I haven't decided yet. He hasn't offered yet."

"She's a fucking person," Dirk snapped. "Not cash or diamonds."

"She's more valuable than both," I said. "And let's not pretend this isn't how the real world works. You should both be happy I'm the one who has her and not someone else. Trust me, it could be much, much worse."

"No," Case said. "I can't imagine anyone worse than you."

———

I HAD private quarters at the Underground, so I stayed there for the night.

I didn't intend to come home for several days.

Tomorrow evening, I would hit Hunter Reyes when he least expected it. That would take some time. I got into bed, the bed where I screwed most of my whores, and I stared at the ceiling as the sunrise started to pierce the curtains.

It was almost six in the morning.

My phone on my nightstand started to ring.

It was Cassini.

I answered, smiling because I knew exactly why she was calling. "Baby."

"When are you coming home?" Exhaustion was in her voice, like she hadn't slept at all. She was probably on the couch in her usual spot.

I liked the way she said *home*, that she considered my building to be her residence. "I don't know."

"What do you mean, you don't know?"

"It might be a few days." I was enjoying this so much.

"Why? Are you okay?"

"I'm fine. I'm sleeping at the Underground."

"I don't understand. Why don't you just come home?"

"Because this is your punishment."

The line went dead silent. She processed the horrifying news without conjuring a response.

She claimed she hated me, but she hated it more when I was gone. She felt vulnerable without my presence, without my ability to drive away the monsters. She didn't know my twin was just one floor below, so if anything happened, he was right there. "I'll be home in a few days." I hung up.

She called back.

My smile was wider now. "Yes?"

"Don't hang up on me."

"Or what?"

I could feel her flames over the line. "Because I said so. And are you being serious right now? You're just going to leave me here?"

"I just put groceries in the fridge."

"That's not the problem."

"You should have thought of that before you pulled your little stunt." She thought she'd outsmarted me with her lingerie, but I always had the upper hand. She got some time with her brothers, but now I would use her own weakness against her. She'd be uncomfortable until I finally walked through the door and chased her fears away. "I'll see you in a few days."

"Like, how many days? Two? Three?"

"I don't know. Between two and six."

"Six is almost a week."

"But not quite."

"What if I just leave?" she countered. "I could storm out of here and take off."

"You're welcome to try, but my men have their orders. If you try to leave, they'll just drag you back up the elevator."

She sighed into the phone. "This is just cruel."

"Well, I'm a cruel man. Goodnight, baby."

"Don't you dare hang up on—"

Click.

13

BALTO

I stayed at the Underground and prepared for our mission to catch Hunter Reyes off guard. He had a place in Tuscany, surrounded by stone walls and gardens for privacy. He produced his product there, hiding in plain sight. Tourists drove past the house and snapped pictures because the property was so beautiful, but they had no idea what sinister things lived inside.

My men wore bulletproof vests, but I hardly ever did. As the Skull King, I had to appear as menacing as possible. It was much more terrifying to be provoked by a man who was fearless, who was so unintimidated that he showed up without any protection. Even in the direst situations, I wore a smile on my face and pretended the whole thing was a joke. It was unnerving. I was a man unafraid of death, and it made provoking my enemies that much more fun.

I watched my men ready the vehicles with all the weapons we would need. We prepared for a full-scale war even though it was just a friendly checkup. I hoped I wouldn't have to execute Hunter tonight. The man made me a lot of money. It would be a shame to break his skull because he was too greedy to pay his share.

My phone started to ring.

Cassini hadn't called me again, probably because she'd figured out she wouldn't be getting her way. I glanced at the scream and hoped to see her name, but it was a number I didn't recognize.

It could be anyone.

I stepped away from the men and moved to the opposite side of the underground garage. I held the phone to my ear. "Balto." I stared at the wall with my arm resting by my side, knowing these phone calls could be declarations of war or just bullshit. At a moment's notice, my life could completely change. In my line of business, the fighting was never really over. One enemy was subdued, and then another popped up.

There was a long pause before his obnoxious voice came over the line. He didn't have a man's voice, a deep baritone that oozed with masculinity. He sounded like a slimy weasel coated with oil. "My maid went through Cassini's things...and discovered she had two phones."

I knew where this was going before he even provided a thorough explanation. My smile was impossible to fight as I imagined his horror when he realized what had transpired right underneath his nose. He was pissed I took his wife and fucked her, but how pissed would he be when he realized I'd been fucking her for much longer? "Maybe she needed a bigger data plan."

Lucian's attitude was still icy. "How long?"

"Does it matter?"

"Yes. It fucking matters."

"When you thought her pussy was wet for you, it was actually wet for me. I'll leave it at that." Torturing this man was almost boring because it was so easy, but I enjoyed it nonetheless. He'd made the biggest mistake of his life when he crossed me. Now I would torture him for as long as possible until it stopped entertaining me. Once I had everything I wanted, including his balls in my hand, I'd finally execute him. Men assumed death was the worst punishment, but that was false. Death was a beautiful, merciful thing. When the body was broken beyond repair and the pain was unbearable, death was the ultimate painkiller. Only healthy people feared death. The broken worshiped it.

Lucian was quiet for a long time, probably because I'd just slapped him with my words.

"Give me what I want, and I might give her back to you."

"I'm not giving you a damn thing. But I will get her back anyway."

"Good luck with that." I'd like to see him try. It would be impossible to break through my power and defenses, but it would be comical to see him make the attempt. "The longer you draw this out, the more fun it is for me."

"The fun is about to stop."

"I don't know about that. Every night I'm having the time of my life—deep inside your wife. By the way, she's got the tightest pussy. You must really miss her." I wanted to taunt him as much as possible, to torture him in every way I could.

There was no rebuttal he could make to a crass comment like that, so he did the only thing he could.

He hung up.

WHEN WE WERE A MILE AWAY, I made the call.

It rang a few times before Hunter answered. Judging by his bubbly tone, he had no idea I was about to arrive at his property with a dozen Hummers and sixty armed men. "Balto, what a nice surprise."

"Yes, I hope it is a nice surprise. I've decided to stop by for a visit. I'll arrive at your gates in less than a minute. The doors better be open by the time I arrive. Understood?" I wasn't stopping by for a chat over a glass of scotch. I had strong reason to believe this man crossed me, betrayed the Skull Kings so he could stuff more cash into his pockets. That was something I couldn't allow.

Hunter's enthusiasm dialed way down. "And the purpose of this surprise visit?"

"Irrelevant." We arrived at the driveway, and I was pleased to see the gates had just been opened. I hung up and stared out the window as we drove farther up the long driveway. Men were posted everywhere, working to load a gray van near the fountain.

I spotted Hunter in front of his house, clearly unnerved by my formidable arrival. Hummer after Hummer pulled into the roundabout, full of armed men with enough ammunition to tear this entire place apart.

If Hunter were smart, he would assume I knew about his little ploy.

My Hummer stopped and I hopped out, my men doing the same. They held their rifles with bulletproof vests strapped across their chests. All I had was the pistol tucked into the back of my jeans.

Hunter stared at me, his blue eyes focused and defensive. His arms hung by his sides, and his pistol was visible on his hip. He surveyed the scene in front of him with a powerful face, but there was no denying the tightness of his facial features. The lights posted around the property made everything easily visible. We got lucky we'd arrived just when they put the product into the van for distribution.

My shoes crunched against the gravel as I made my way toward him. The sound of each step filled the tense silence. When I reached him, I could see just how annoyed he was. Minutes ago, he was carefree and happy. But now he knew he was in serious shit. "Hunter."

"Balto." He stepped closer to me and placed his hands on his hips. "This is quite an entrance."

"Skull Kings are a bit dramatic. But effective." I glanced at the van then looked back at him. There were over a hundred men on the property, all armed and waiting for whatever would happen next. We outnumbered them three to one, so it wasn't in their best interest to pull the trigger first. "The month's stash is in there?"

Hunter kept his gaze on me. "Yes. You'll get your money like you always do."

"But will I get all of it?"

Hunter's jaw tightened.

"You're a good guy, Hunter. You make an excellent product and don't cause any trouble. I don't like people much, but I think I like you. I want to keep liking you...but that depends on what happens next."

Hunter took the high road by staying silent. If he said

the wrong thing now, it could be the last words he ever spoke.

"How much is in there?" I nodded to the van.

"At least twenty million."

I crossed my arms over my chest. "Since we've been working together for so long, I'll give you a chance. One of my men informed me that you're misreporting your earnings, cutting my share significantly. Is there any truth to that statement?"

Hunter didn't blurt out the answer I wanted to hear. He stayed silent for a while, trying to figure out what to do.

"A man who owns up to his mistakes is redeemable. But a man who lies..." I shook my head. "He's worthless. I suggest you think about your answer carefully and be prepared to live with it...or die for it." Criminal men got greedy all the time. I didn't like to kill the ones who were productive, so if he told me the truth, I'd knock his teeth out but allow him to live. If he lied to me...there was no going back. For his sake and mine, I hoped he went for the truth.

"No."

My eyes narrowed slightly, disappointed with the answer.

"I don't know who told you that, but they're full of shit. We've been working together for—"

"Open the van."

"Why?"

"Open the fucking van." I marched to the gray van with no windows and snapped my fingers. My men appeared with a large crowbar and popped the back door open. Both doors were pulled open and revealed the stash of drugs perfectly wrapped in their plastic containers. Piled from the floor to the ceiling, there was much more than twenty million worth. It had to be at least five times that amount. I walked back to Hunter.

"I'm not exactly sure how much is in there," Hunter blurted. "It's just a guess—"

"You expect me to believe that a man such as yourself is so careless that he doesn't know if he as a hundred million worth of drugs or twenty? Now you're just insulting me." I released a loud whistle.

Two of my men grabbed Hunter by both arms and pinned him to the ground, forcing his head against the concrete.

"I'm sorry, alright?" Hunter tried to fight their hold, but he was outnumbered.

All my men had their weapons focused on his army. None of his men wanted to die, so they didn't retaliate. They didn't defend their leader on the ground because it was a battle they couldn't possibly win.

"I admit it," Hunter said. "I lied. But I won't do it again. I'm sorry. I'm fucking sorry." Panic caused his voice to turn high-pitched. Full of terror and fear, he started to sound like a little girl who didn't want a spanking.

"I gave you a chance, Hunter. You blew it."

"You put me on the spot—"

I slammed my foot hard onto his skull.

He screamed at the contact, his head thudding against the concrete from the impact.

I slammed my foot again and again until the screaming stopped. Then it was just the sound of his skull cracking under my boot. It took a few stomps, but soon his brains were smeared across the concrete and blood dripped into the grass.

When he was dead, I wiped my shoes on the grass then walked up to the first man I saw. "You're in charge now. Take care of the shipment and keep the operation going. Cross me—and the same thing will happen to your skull."

14

CASSINI

Four days came and went, and Balto didn't come home.

It was a cruel punishment.

At first, I was relieved that he wouldn't hurt me, but then I realized there were things worse than physical pain.

Like being locked in a tower.

I spent my time reading, watching TV, and eating everything he left for me in the fridge. Time passed so slowly, but I refused to call him because I was too proud. I'd tried to get some leverage over him, but he continued to hang up on me.

Fucking bastard.

A mischievous idea came to mind, so I pulled on a new piece of lingerie and stood in front of the full-length mirror. I snapped a few pictures before I texted them to Balto. *Look at what you're missing.*

The three dots never appeared.

He never texted me back.

Jackass.

I sat in the living room and waited for the time to pass. He had to come back eventually, as much as he enjoyed torturing me. I didn't just feel vulnerable, but I felt neglected, like a dog that had been abandoned.

Next time, I would think twice before pissing him off. He definitely served me a cold dish of revenge.

The elevator beeped, and my heart nearly jumped out of my chest. It'd been four painfully long days, and now he was finally back. I should be too pissed to be excited, but I was relieved I wouldn't be alone in this building any longer. The strongest man I'd ever laid eyes on had just returned to the fortress. Now I didn't have to worry about all the evil men who wanted to do terrible things to me. Balto was like a scarecrow—he could chase all the birds away.

I rose to my feet to greet him, wearing his boxers that were rolled a dozen times to stay on my hips. I wore one of my camisoles without a bra, lounging around the house because I had nothing else to do.

The elevator doors opened and revealed the man I'd missed every moment since he left. With the same blue eyes, sharp cheekbones, and powerful shoulders, he was a beautiful man. He stepped inside, looked me up and down, and then whistled. "Damn. Look at those legs." He was in a blue t-shirt and black jeans, and his muscular arms stretched the cotton. He approached me, his eyes devouring me like he'd never seen me before. "I would love to feel them wrapped around my head."

The excitement slowly drained from my veins when I detected something different about him. It looked just like him, everything identical. But that smile was different. The choice of words was different. Balto was a man of few words and rarely complimented me like that. If he really wanted me, he just grabbed me by the hair and took me. His eyes didn't roam with desire. There was never any time for that.

He stopped right in front of me and dragged the backs of his fingers down my arm, starting from the shoulder and moving to my wrist. He watched his hand glide over my body, as if he'd never touched me before.

Balto had not had a change in personality since I met him. He was always exactly the same, even when he was angry. With little emotion, he was a simple man. But this man was so identical, he had to be the man I'd been waiting for.

"You are beautiful, sweetheart." His fingers moved to my hair, and he gently felt the strands.

My eyes widened in alarm because Balto had never called me that. He used a very different nickname and never deviated from his choice. I glanced at his right hand and noticed the iconic ring was missing, the skull diamond he never took off. He wore it to bed and in the shower. He told me he never removed it. If he didn't have it on him now, then it was missing. And if it was missing, he'd be angrier than a hurricane.

So this couldn't be him.

I stepped back. "Don't touch me."

His hand remained in the air where he'd been touching my strands. His eyebrow rose, but his smile didn't falter. "I don't bite."

"Well, I do. Get out."

"Wow, you really do have an attitude." He stepped forward even when I stepped back.

"Yes, especially when I have a weapon." I snatched the

lamp sitting on the end table and yanked the cord out of the socket. The base was heavy, so it should do some real damage.

He watched me, amused by my rage. "I hope you have something better than a lamp."

"My nails dig in pretty deep."

"Ooh." He waggled his eyebrows. "That's more my style."

I held the lamp at the ready, prepared to smack him upside the head if he came too close. "Who are you?"

"You don't recognize me, sweetheart?"

"Don't make me ask you again." He had the same baritone voice, dripping with masculinity, and he had the exact same features. His size was similar, his frame packed with muscle. But I knew this wasn't the man I was sleeping with. Balto mentioned he had a brother—but not a twin. "I know you aren't Balto, so stop pretending."

He dropped his smile then raised both hands in surrender. "Sweetheart, calm down. I'm not gonna hurt you."

"No, it seems like you want to do something *else* to me." Even when he lowered his hands, I kept the lamp at the ready.

He rolled his eyes. "I didn't expect you to be dressed like that when I walked in. Caught me off guard, alright? I've got a weak spot for a woman in a thin camisole with no bra. Sexy as hell. Can't blame me for that."

"You shouldn't have barged in."

"It's not like there's a doorbell. So calm down. That lamp is worthless, so put it down."

"I'll put it down when you leave."

He rolled his eyes then pulled a gun from the back of his jeans. "Look, if I wanted to hurt you—"

Instinctively, I struck the gun with the lamp and sent it flying across the room.

His head snapped in the direction of the flying gun, shocked that I'd smacked it out of his hands so quickly.

Before he could run and snatch it, I hit him upside the head with the lamp, shattering the glass on impact.

"Jesus!" He fell to the floor, the shards surrounding him.

I picked up the gun from the ground and clicked off the safety button. With both hands, I pointed the barrel right at the intruder, prepared to kill him if I had to. "Now who the hell are you?"

He wiped the blood from his forehead with his hand and admired the red substance. "Shit, you got me good."

"And I can get you good again." I cocked the gun.

He rose to his feet but didn't seem the least bit scared of the weapon in my hand. "Who do you think I am, sweetheart? I'm Balto's brother."

"Stop calling me sweetheart."

"Why? It's cute—as are you."

I stepped forward. "I will shoot you."

"Fine. Just not the face. I need that to get laid."

I lowered the gun and pointed it between his legs. "Then maybe I should shoot here."

"Balto wasn't kidding. You're definitely a handful."

I nodded to the elevator. "Get out. I don't know how you got in here in the first place, but I'll make sure you don't come back."

He cocked an eyebrow. "You don't know how I got in here? Seriously, Balto didn't tell you?"

"Balto didn't tell me what?"

"Man, he really is ashamed of me, huh?" He shook his head. "That asshole."

I held the gun steady and tried not to be distracted by his words. It could all be a ploy for me to lose my concentration.

"I only came up here to introduce myself. You've been alone for like four days, so I thought you could use the company."

My finger remained on the trigger. "You call that an introduction? You complimented my legs then dragged your fingers down my arm."

"Again, you're a beautiful woman. I had a momentarily lapse in judgment. You should take it as a compliment. Besides, I've been in prison for the last six months. All I can think about is women."

Good thing I had the gun. "I wonder why Balto didn't mention you...when you're so delightful."

"I am delightful. We just got off on the wrong foot."

"I'm about to shoot you in the foot." I changed my aim to his shoe.

"Sweetheart, I can tell you've never fired a gun in your life. So just put it down—"

"Just because I've never fired one of these things doesn't mean I won't do it now. So get the hell out and—"

The elevator beeped, and the doors began to open.

The man sighed. "Great...just great."

That could only be one person, so I was relieved.

The doors opened fully, and Balto stepped inside. Dressed in all black, he looked like he'd spent the evening executing people. A bag was over his shoulder as he stopped in the entryway and stared at the scene in front of him.

I still had the gun pointed at his twin, and the broken lamp was still in pieces on the floor.

His brother tried to brush off the situation. "It's not as bad as it looks."

"It's exactly as bad as it looks," I snapped. "He just barged in here and ran his fingers down my arm. He told me I had beautiful legs then touched my hair."

Balto turned his expression on his brother, his features not changing, but his mood darkening. Without blinking, he stared him down, his body so still he seemed to be made of stone.

I lowered the gun because it felt unnecessary to keep my aim.

Balto slowly walked toward his brother. "Is that true?"

I clicked the safety on then set the gun on the table. It didn't seem like I needed it anymore.

The man held Balto's gaze, his nostrils flaring as he sighed. "Yes, but—"

Balto punched him so hard that he collapsed to the ground. Even with his large size, Balto moved with impressive speed. Like a snake that launched at its prey, the attack was so fast that I didn't even see it.

He stayed on the ground for a few seconds, his eyes blinking as he recovered from the hit. "I came to introduce myself…but got sidetracked by her outfit. It was a dick thing to do, but also harmless."

"Stand up so I can hit you again."

"This wouldn't have happened if you'd just introduced us like I asked."

"And this shit is exactly why I didn't introduce you. Now stand up like a man or be kicked like a dog. Which do you prefer?"

He rolled his eyes before he rose to his full height again.

Balto hit him again, sending him back to the floor.

I actually felt bad for his brother. That looked painful.

"We done yet?" his brother asked as he got to his feet.

"I told you not to come up here."

"You left the woman alone for four days—"

"She's my woman, and I can do whatever the fuck I want." He grabbed him by the throat and squeezed his fingers around his windpipe. "My absence doesn't give you the right to march in here and touch her like she's yours. Asshole, she's mine. If you were someone else, I would have already killed you. But if you do it again, I *will* kill you." He released his grip.

The man rubbed his throat but refused to cough. "No touching. Got it."

Balto finally turned around and looked at me. There was no longing in his eyes like he'd missed me. He seemed just as angry at me as he was with his brother. "Are you alright?"

"I'm fine." I crossed my arms over my chest, hiding my tits from view. The shirt was thin and sheer, so I was practically on display.

"Are you satisfied with his punishment?"

"What does that mean?" I asked.

"Do you want me to keep hurting him?" Balto asked. "Because I will."

The guy probably had a concussion, so I thought he'd been punished enough. "I'm satisfied."

He turned back to his brother. "Cassini, this is Heath. My twin."

Heath raised a hand in acknowledgment. "Wonderful to meet you."

"Not so wonderful to meet you," I said coldly.

"He's in the building because he lives on the third floor," Balto explained. "I let him live there until he got back on his feet. But now that he's broken one of my only rules, he'll be moving elsewhere."

"Come on, I just wanted to check in on the girl," Heath argued. "I didn't come off very well, but my intentions were good. Don't kick me out."

"You can afford something else." Balto left his brother's side and examined the shards on the floor. Then he walked toward me.

"I know I can afford to move. But I like it here. Doesn't it make sense for both of us to be in the same place? If we're ever attacked, I've always got you and you've always got me."

"It would have made sense before you pissed me off." Balto's eyes moved over my hands and arms to make sure I didn't have any injuries. He grabbed the gun off the table then tossed it at his brother. "Now apologize to Cassini and get the fuck out."

Heath slipped the gun into the back of his jeans then walked up to me. "Sorry, sweetheart—"

"Don't call me that."

He did his best to hide his smile. "Alright. Sorry about this all this. I'll be on my best behavior from now on. You know, so Balto doesn't rip out my throat."

I stared at him in silence, not ready to accept his apology. "You should be on your best behavior so I don't shoot you. Because I will."

He couldn't stop himself from smiling that time. His eyes glanced up to meet Balto's. "I like her." Heath walked to the elevator then disappeared.

When he was really gone, I turned to look at Balto, finally appreciating the fact that he was there. The second he walked through those doors, he made all my problems go away. He turned into a deranged pit bull and scared off my assailant.

"That won't happen again." He stuck his right hand into my hair and cradled the back of my head as he looked into my face. "But he is harmless, just to give you peace of mind."

"He said he just got out of prison."

"Because I put him there. He was doing petty crimes and pissing off the police. I put him there to straighten him out."

"You can do that?" I asked in surprise.

"Baby, I can do anything." He tilted my head slightly so he could lean in and kiss me softly on the mouth.

I'd missed that kiss over these last four days. My longing outweighed my rage, so I forgot that I was pissed at him.

"How did you know he wasn't me?"

"It was easy."

His fingers glided to my neck, and his thumb rested in the corner of my mouth. "Hardly anyone can tell us apart. How did you manage?"

"You may look alike, but you're nothing alike. The second he opened his mouth, I knew something was off. He complimented my legs, but that's something you wouldn't do. If you found me attractive, you would just take me. He kept calling me sweetheart...something you've never called me. And he wasn't wearing your ring. I figured it out in thirty seconds."

Approval shone in his eyes. "How did you get his gun?"

"I knocked it out of his hands, hit him in the head with the lamp, then took it."

"Maybe I underestimated you." His hands moved down to my waist, his large arms circling me until I was cradled against his chest.

"Of course you did."

"It was sexy watching you point that gun at him. I like a woman who puts a man in his place."

"I'll put you in your place soon enough."

The corner of his mouth rose in a smile as he pulled me closer. "I'm a man who can never be put in his place. But I welcome you to try." He kissed the corner of my mouth before he released me.

"Did you get the pictures I sent?"

"Why do you think I came home?" He grabbed his bag off the table and carried it to his bedroom. "But then I walked in on a scene from the *Godfather*. Got a bit distracted."

I followed him into his bedroom and watched him set his bag on the dresser. "I'm glad the punishment is finally over."

"I hope you learned your lesson."

"I did. But don't expect me to behave myself."

He tossed his clothes in the hamper then set his bag in

the closet. "Every time you piss me off, I'll be gone longer... and longer."

Now he'd just raised the stakes, and I didn't want to play his games anymore. Four days already felt like an eternity. Eight days would feel like hell. Anything longer than that would just be cruel. "What did you do while you were gone?" Did he sleep alone every night? Was he surrounded by women who wanted to dig their claws into him? Why did I care?

He pulled his shirt over his head and tossed it into the hamper. "You should trust me. I'm a man of my word."

"I never said I didn't."

He undid the top of his jeans and got them off. "I can read you better than you realize."

He must have been telling the truth because he was right on the money. "Four nights is a long time to be alone."

"Nothing my hand can't fix." He tossed his jeans into the hamper and stood in just his boxers, six-three of nothing but muscle and man. "And what did you do while I was gone?"

"Watched TV...read a book...ate a lot."

"Touch yourself?"

I brushed off the question by tucking my hair behind my ear.

He grinned. "Admit it or deny it, I already know the answer."

"I wouldn't have to do that if you were here."

"Well, you forced my hand. Don't let it happen again." He grabbed the bottom of my camisole and pulled it over my head, revealing my bare tits with their hard nipples. His hands palmed both of them, and he moaned, like playing with my tits felt as good as getting a massage.

"You never answered my question."

He grabbed the top of my boxers then pushed them over my hips, revealing the bright teal thong. He lowered himself to his knees as he peeled both away, his lips caressing my thighs at the same time. "You really want to know? Or do you want to be full of my come while I tell you?" He rose to his feet again, and his hands returned to my tits. He rested his mouth close to mine and guided me back toward the bed.

All my anger and resentment faded away when this beautiful man wanted me. His powerful chest was hypnotic, and it'd been so long since his fat dick was inside me. Just like when we were lovers, I didn't care about anything going on in real life. I just wanted to get lost in the passion, the ecstasy. "I want your come inside me…"

15

CASSINI

He thrust inside me while his arms were pinned behind my knees. He'd already taken me several times, but he got hard again almost instantly and we were back at it. I was full of his come, but I was about to take another load. "Ready for more?" His blue eyes burned into mine as he kept rocking into me, getting his entire length inside me with every thrust. Long and fat, he had the kind of dick that always pleased a woman. He was anatomically built for pleasure.

"Yes." My hands dug into his hair, and my body pressed back into the mattress every time he dug in deep inside me. I let this man have me, let him take all of me. He'd already made me explode enough times to make up for the last four days, and now I wanted him to enjoy his final bliss. "Give it to me." My hand gripped his ass and I yanked on him, pulling him hard inside me.

He moaned as he finished, giving me another load that couldn't possibly fit with all the others. His dick throbbed as it released, and all the muscles in his powerful body tightened in response. He looked me in the eye as he finished, making the sexiest bedroom eyes as he clenched his jaw in a rugged way.

I loved feeling him fill me. I never enjoyed it so much with another man. Every time he emptied himself in my pussy it was like having a micro-orgasm. I loved watching him feel pleasure, loved seeing him experience the same high I received.

When his cock started to soften, he pulled out.

The come dripped everywhere.

He admired it before he rolled over and lay on his back.

Now it was evening, around the time I would normally go to sleep. I hadn't been sleeping well with him gone, so I knew I would crash hard tonight.

He stayed on his side of the bed as the sweat evaporated from his skin. Slowly, his breathing returned to normal, and he closed his eyes as he relaxed.

I pulled the sheets to my shoulders and turned on my side, so comfortable that I could fall asleep that very moment. But my eyes stayed open so I could look at him, admire all those muscles. Even when he was relaxed, he was still so tight.

He must have felt me staring at him because he turned his head to look at me. "Like what you see?"

Instead of being a smartass, I told the truth. "Yes. You're the most beautiful man I've ever seen."

He stared at me without blinking. "I never get compliments from you."

"Because you don't need to hear them." He knew I

wanted him, always had. Every time I tried to call things off, he knew it would never happen. I would call him again and again because I was so addicted.

He turned his head and looked at the ceiling. "You're the most beautiful woman I've ever seen."

I knew he'd been with more women than I could probably count, so I found that unlikely. But he said he wouldn't lie, not even to spare my feelings. He was transparent in his thoughts, saying exactly what he felt. So if he said it, he must mean it. "I find that hard to believe. There's a lot of competition out there."

"No, there's not." He moved his arm underneath his head for more support, the sheets bunched around his waist. "I may have been with a lot of women, but that doesn't mean they were special. I'm the kind of man that just wants sex, so I'm not picky with my partners. As long as they've got tits and ass, it doesn't make a difference to me."

"If it matters so little, then why don't you just jerk off?"

"Because I like tits and ass a lot more than my hand."

For a man so handsome and rich, he could have any woman he wanted. He could buy a beautiful woman and make her his, exactly the way Lucian did with me. But just like with his beat-up truck, he didn't seem to care about the finer things in life. "And you really think I'm the most beautiful woman you've ever seen?"

"I said it, didn't I?" His hand rested across his stomach. "I don't say things I don't mean."

"Is that why this has lasted so long?"

He took a quiet breath, considering his answer. "Partially. But a lot of it has to do with who your husband is."

"But you had no idea who he was for the first month."

He was quiet again, choosing his answer carefully. "Then that was all you."

Had he been with anyone else during that time? Was I the only one? Was he as obsessed with me as I was with him? "Were you with anyone else during that time?" It was unfair for me to care about sharing him, not when I had still been sleeping with my husband. I'd waited for the agony to end so I could retreat to my bedroom and wash his scent away. Just to get through it, I pictured the man I really wanted, even though Lucian's smaller size made that difficult to pretend.

"Does it matter?"

"I was just curious."

When he was quiet, it was obvious he wasn't going to give me an answer.

"I thought you were always honest."

"I am always honest." His voice was rough like the hardwood of an ancient tree. He had so much strength in just the tone of his voice. Unnatural levels of testosterone made him so male. "Did I tell you a lie?"

"No. But why won't you answer?"

"Because it's none of your business. That's why."

His cold dismissal made me quiet, but it also made me curious. If he had been with other women, he wouldn't care about hurting my feelings. It wouldn't change our relationship since he didn't owe me anything. So why would he not just tell me? "You weren't."

He slowly turned his head my way, staring at me with those cold eyes.

"You said you didn't care about hurting my feelings, so

you would just tell me if there had been others. I have no right to be upset anyway. I was still with Lucian at the time...even though I hated it. So the only reason why you aren't answering is because there was no one else...and you don't want me to know that."

He had the best poker face in the world, an expression that was flat like a slab of concrete and cold like the winter winds. His thoughts were buried under his hostility. If he were my opponent across a battlefield, I'd shit my pants. He turned his head back to the ceiling. "One of the men under my ranks crossed me. Hunter Reyes has been one of my top drug dealers for the last few years. Always pulls in great numbers and stays out of my way. But one of my spies informed me that Hunter's been skimming off the top, underreporting the amount of product he's shipping, and therefore, undercutting my fee."

I still wanted to press him for an answer, but I became so engrossed in his tale that I pushed it into the back of my mind. This sounded like a story that would lead to a war—with lots of causalities.

"I took sixty of my best men and confronted him on his doorstep. He had just transferred the product into the back of his van. I pride myself on being a fair and just Skull King. I don't execute a man unless I'm positive that he's guilty. And if he is guilty, depending on the severity of the crime, I always extend a less cruel punishment—if they earn it. But they have to be honest with me, look me in the eye and tell me exactly what they did. Unfortunately, Hunter Reyes insulted me by expecting me to buy his bullshit. He actually thought he could trick me and get away with it. It was disrespectful...and I can't stand disrespect. So I broke into the van and caught him red-handed."

This story didn't have a happy ending. "What did you do?"

"I crushed his skull under my boot."

My hand immediately went to my mouth as I silenced a gasp. The mental image popped into my head, a man begging for his life while this behemoth stomped his shoe so hard that it shattered his skull. Blood and brains must have spilled everywhere. It was a violent and painful death, so disturbing that it nearly made me sick.

"Don't feel bad for him. I gave him a way out—and he didn't take it."

"What if he had told you the truth?"

"I would have beaten him to within an inch of his life—but he would have lived. He gave me no choice. My men respect me, and I can never lose that admiration. If I granted this man mercy, it would have made me weak. I didn't want to grant him mercy anyway, so it didn't matter. A man who crosses me like that doesn't deserve to live. He deserves to be tortured and humiliated in front of his men."

It took me a few seconds to recover from the tale, to understand what this man was truly capable of.

"Another reason I despise Lucian. He hides behind his bombs and explosives and detonates them when he's safe somewhere else. When he kills his enemies, he has one of his men do it for him. The man isn't a man at all. He's just a genius with a fat wallet. That doesn't impress me."

Nothing about Lucian impressed me. "His men don't admire him. They're just afraid of him."

"That's not leadership."

It was crazy to believe that this warlord had so much nobility and class when he was a murderer and a criminal. He was just and merciful. He never lied. He was transparent and respectable. He didn't seem to care about money either, so why didn't he pursue a different line of work?

"I respect your brothers. And respect is hard to earn from me."

The mention of my family made me forget about Lucian.

"They came to the Underground, surrounded by hundreds of the biggest criminals in this city, and not once did they show their fear. They offered me everything they had if I let you go."

My eyes closed as the emotion hit, thinking about my brothers willing to give up their pasta company just so they could have me back. My brothers were so fearless, especially Case. There was nothing they wouldn't do for me— and I loved them from the bottom of my heart. "I'm guessing you said no."

"Baby, I'll never say yes."

The hope left my heart.

"But I admire them for trying. I admire them for sacrificing everything for you. I sincerely hope I never have to kill them."

"Kill them and I'll kill you." The words flew out of my mouth by their own will. I wouldn't take them back because I meant them so passionately. I knew that I had feelings for this man, that I was in his bed because I wanted to be, not had to be. I even respected him. But if I ever had to choose, there was no question who I would choose.

The corner of his mouth rose in a smile. "Just when I thought I was satisfied, you say something like that...and I want you all over again."

"I mean it. I'm not bluffing."

"I know...and that's why it's so sexy."

16

BALTO

I always woke up before Cassini, so I changed my clothes and headed to the gym on the first floor.

Heath was there. With headphones over his ears while he did bicep curls with a heavy bar, sweat was marked across his brow and his neck. His lips were pressed tightly together as he pumped out his reps.

Just looking at him pissed me off.

Heath racked his bar when he noticed me. "Still pissed—"

I slammed my fist into his face.

He stumbled back slightly then wiped the blood that dripped from his nose. "I'll take that as a yes..."

"I told you my place was off-limits, and you didn't listen to me."

"You left her alone for four days—"

"Doesn't fucking matter. If she needed something, she could call me. She doesn't need some asshole barging in there pretending to be me."

"I wasn't pretending to be you. I was just having a bit of fun...but she didn't fall for it."

Because the woman really knew me. She knew how I looked at her, how I spoke to her, and how I treated her. It was an indirect line of loyalty that she showed me. My brother and I looked identical so she had to be attracted to him, but she didn't hesitate to smash a glass lamp over his head and pull a gun on him. It was clear exactly where her commitment was. "Because she knows who she's sleeping with."

"Come on, you know I wouldn't have done anything if she actually thought I was you."

"Because I would have killed you."

"No," he corrected. "Because that woman actually means something to you."

"Yet, you don't hesitate to stare at her legs and imagine them wrapped around your head."

Heath shrugged. "She's a beautiful woman. What do you want me to say? I'm a man, and you can't expect me not to think like a man."

"But I can expect you to behave like a brother. I warned you if you had a mishap, I'd throw you back in that hellhole."

"That was work-related, not personally related."

"Same thing to me."

He wiped away the last few drops of blood before he crossed his arms over his chest. "I apologized. Can we move on?"

I knew my brother wouldn't have crossed the line more than he did. His behavior wasn't acceptable, but it wasn't unforgivable. Cassini looked so sexy in that thin top and boxers that I could hardly blame him. "Don't do that again."

"You have my word."

"And don't go up there again."

He nodded. "Fine. But what if I need to talk to her?"

"Why would you need to talk to her?"

"I don't know, because we're neighbors? Because she's my brother's girlfriend? Because—"

"She's not my girlfriend." I kept my voice simple, but my tone deepened. I hated that phrase, that label. It was a term teenagers used. I was no teenager. I was a fucking man. I was a Skull King. The only phrase that actually meant something to me was wife—and I would never have a wife. A woman was either nothing or something. There was no in-between.

"Then what is she?"

"A woman I'm fucking."

Heath rolled his eyes. "Whatever you say. You've never fucked a single woman for two months."

"But I've never been with the wife of my enemy."

He shook his head. "You were fucking her long before that. You can pretend that's the reason, but we both know that's bullshit. She knows it's bullshit too."

"She said that?" If that woman suspected she actually meant something to me, I had a serious problem on my hands. She didn't press me on my bedroom activities before I'd realized she was married to Lucian. She must have suspected I hadn't been with anyone else, but I just didn't want to admit it. She was wasting her time because I would never confess to that.

"No, but that's a smart woman. She knocked the gun out

of my hand, slammed that lamp on my head, and then pointed the barrel right at my face. I brushed it off at the time, but it was fucking impressive. She thinks quick on her feet. And she's got one hell of a mouth on her. I was only around her for a few minutes, but I understand your obsession."

When the doors had opened and I observed the scene in front of me, there was definitely a glow of pride inside my chest. Heath was a strong man with quick reflexes, but my woman managed to put him in his place. It didn't seem like I needed to give him a worse punishment.

"So can I have a relationship with the woman?"

"She doesn't want one with you."

"I can win her over. You obviously did."

"I've never pulled a stunt like that."

"No, but I'm sure you've done much worse." He stepped closer to me. "If this woman is going to be around for the long haul, we need to bury the hatchet and form an alliance. Lucian will try to take her at some point, and if I'm here and you aren't, it's my responsibility to keep her safe. I'm the last line of defense."

I couldn't argue with that. "She doesn't like you, Heath."

"She didn't like you either, and she's fucking your brains out."

"Not the same thing."

"Let me take her out to dinner—"

"Not gonna happen." Some other guy wasn't taking my woman anywhere.

"Then convince her to come down for a drink. I wanna make nice, alright?"

"Why is this so important to you?" My brother never

cared whether someone liked him or not. He never cared about making amends with someone he wronged. He did whatever he wanted without thinking about anyone but himself. Why was Cassini any different?

He lowered his arms and prepared to turn away. "Because she's important to you, brother."

FALL WAS NOW APPROACHING WINTER, and the air was noticeably colder. When I worked late at night, there was always frost on my windshield when I left it in the garage all night. Now I wore long-sleeved shirts and light jackets when I left the house. Dressed in a black leather jacket and a white V-neck shirt, I was ready to take Cassini to visit with her brothers.

She came down the hallway, dressed in black leggings, tan booties, and a maroon sweater that covered her ass. Her hair was curled, and she wore the hoop earrings I bought for her. My personal shopper did a great job dressing her, finding the perfect clothes to amplify her stunning beauty. I preferred the short dresses where her cleavage was visible, but even when she was completely covered, she was still the sexiest thing in the world. "Morning."

"It's noon."

"That's morning to me." She helped herself to a mug of coffee before she sat across from me. She skipped her meal because she didn't usually eat first thing in the morning. She usually watched me eat my boring breakfast of fish or egg whites. "Since you keep me up so late..." She brought the steaming coffee to her lips and took a drink.

"I wouldn't be much of a man if I didn't keep you up late."

She stared into her coffee mug. "Why are you dressed so nice?"

I glanced down at my clothes. "Nice?"

"If you're staying home, you don't really wear much at all. And you hardly go to work during the day. You must have some plans."

"My plans are none of your business."

She lifted her gaze and gave me a cold look. "Let's stop that bullshit right now. If I'm going to live with you however long this takes, you need to stop shutting me down like I don't matter. I do matter—and we both know it. I treat you with respect, so you need to treat me with respect."

"Believe it or not, I do treat you with respect."

"How so?"

"You don't have any bruises, right?" I drank my coffee and watched the fire dance in her eyes. Truth be told, I liked her more when she stood up to me, when she called me out on my bullshit. She was right in being upset. She was also right that I was doing the best I could to make her feel insignificant—because she was very significant.

"That's not respect. That's human decency."

"Well, I'm not a decent human. We both know that."

"I think you're noble, just, and fair. Hitting me wouldn't be fair, and that's why you haven't done it. I also think talking to me like that isn't fair since you and I are committed partners. If this relationship is monogamous, then I have the right to ask where you're going."

I wanted to kiss her when she got all bossy like that. "Wrong. Monogamy means you have the right to ask for my fidelity. It means you have the right to be the only woman I fuck. You own a piece of me—but just a small amount. I own all of you, and you're my prisoner. The rest of me is off-limits."

She set her coffee mug down and leaned forward. "You just cost yourself a night of sex."

The corner of my mouth rose in a smile. "Sure, baby. Whatever you say."

"I mean it."

"All I have to do is pin you down and kiss that delicious pussy of yours, and you'll be begging me to fuck you. Word of advice from an experienced leader, don't make empty threats. It just makes you look weak when you cave." I rose from the table and grabbed my mug. "I'm going to see your brothers today—and you're coming with me."

She looked horrified by the news rather than relieved. "Why didn't you just tell me that in the first place?"

"I would have if you hadn't interrogated me."

"I didn't interrogate you. I just asked a simple question."

"Well, if you didn't ask me at all, I would have told you."

She slammed her mug down on the table. "You need to get off your little power trip and chill out. Establishing power by being an asshole just makes you an asshole. I'm not one of your men, and I'm not your enemy. I understand you don't know how to do that, but you need to figure out another way because these tactics just make you look like a douchebag."

17

BALTO

We drove across the city in my old truck.

She was quiet on her side, saying nothing to me after her little tantrum back at the house.

If someone else spoke to me that way, I would be pissed and lay down the law. But listening to her tell me off and insult me was oddly arousing. Everyone I met was afraid of me, except whores because they knew I was a good-paying customer, and this woman had every reason to be afraid of me—only she wasn't.

She refused to be pushed around and treated with less respect than she deserved.

Reminded me of myself.

The way her green eyes lit up like flames when she was really pissed was so sexy. All I wanted to do was throw her on the table and fuck her into submission. I took this woman as much as I could, but it never made me want her less. It never made me want someone else instead. I refused to admit she was the only one because that would give her way too much power.

The fact that she had any power at all was sexy.

This woman was taking more and more from me without even realizing it.

It'd been thirty minutes since her last spoken word. Now she broke the silence, looking out the window so she wouldn't have to look at me. "Why are we seeing Case and Dirk? Or are you going to refuse to tell me that?"

My mouth raised in a smile, loving her smartass attitude. "It was part of the deal we made."

"And what deal is that?"

"That I would bring you to visit once a week."

"In exchange for?"

"Nothing. I just felt bad for them. Once you earn your freedom from me, you can visit them on your own."

She adopted a whiny, childlike voice as she said, "Once you earn your freedom from me..." Full of sass and annoyance, she mocked me with such disdain.

It only amused me. "I can turn around if you'd like."

That shut her up.

I expected her to make a comment about my old truck, but she never did. She was used to luxury with Lucian, driving a Bugatti herself. My truck still had a CD and cassette player. It was built long before Bluetooth. I'd had it for nearly twelve years, and the transmission was still good. Driving around in an expensive car only increased unwanted attention. And I didn't care about showing off my wealth. The ring on my finger was worth at least a billion euro. There was no vehicle that compared to that.

Cassini didn't seem to care—and that made me like her even more.

We arrived at the factory then walked inside.

"Play nice, alright?" she asked as she looked at me over her shoulder.

"Who brought you here?" I took the lead and made her walk behind me.

We entered the kitchen first, the place where I'd confronted Case the first time. He was there now, wearing a white chef's jacket as he worked on a new recipe. He'd just pulled the pasta out of the boiling pot and placed it in a strainer in the stainless-steel sink.

When he spotted my large frame in the corner of his eye, he met my look. Visibly annoyed and displeased, he didn't hide his disdain from me. That was more apparent when his eyes shifted to his sister. He didn't show a lot of emotion, but just the light changes in his eyes and mouth showed the unconditional love and powerful bond he had for her. Even if he hadn't proven his adoration when he came to the Underground, I would have spotted it now. But he didn't give her any affection, and the look quickly faded away. "Hey, Cassini."

She came around the island and hugged him from the side as he stood at the sink. "I missed you."

He gave her a one-armed hug and kissed her forehead. "I missed you too, *sorella*."

Sister.

"What are you making?" She looked down into the strainer and saw the fettuccini that was still steaming. She picked up a noodle to place in her mouth.

He smacked it away. "Don't be a pig."

"I'm hungry. The only hot meals I get at Balto's place are fish and chicken."

"That doesn't sound so bad to me." He shook the strainer and dropped the pasta into a large bowl.

She stuck out her tongue. "You're both annoying."

He moved back to the stove, where he had sauce cooking in a pan. "I'm trying a new recipe, something a bit spicier. Trying to figure out if it would be better over pasta or stuffed inside lasagna."

"Lasagna," she blurted. "But let's try it anyway."

"Who said this was for you?" he asked with a chuckle.

"Oh, come on," she whined. "I haven't had a home-cooked pasta meal in forever. And where is your Italian hospitality?"

"I'm running a business, not a hospitality service."

"Well, I own a third of that service, so a third of that is mine."

He sighed and smiled at the same time. "Alright. I'll get it ready."

She clapped her hands excitedly. "I knew you'd cave."

Case turned to me. "You want any, Balto?"

"No thanks." I was surprised he even asked. It was unlike an Italian to feed their enemy.

"Yes, he'll have some," Cassini said. "This is the real deal. You aren't going to pass it up because you're afraid of carbs."

Just a few carbs made a big difference. My frame was so muscled and tight because I didn't eat carbs, which meant there weren't any carbs to turn to sugar then to fat. It was the best way to keep this chiseled frame. "I said no—"

"And I said yes." She turned to her brother. "Make him

a plate. I'm going to say hi to Dirk." She headed for the kitchen door. "Don't kill each other while I'm gone."

The door swung shut, and minutes of silence passed afterward.

Case prepared the plates and broke the tension. "To answer your unspoken question, yes, she's always been that bossy."

"I figured." Judging by the way she pushed her brothers around, she'd been that way for a long time.

"Have you reconsidered our offer?" He placed the dirty dishes in the sink to be cleaned later.

"No. And I won't."

He wiped his hands on a towel as he looked at me, his disappointment obvious.

"Just be grateful I've allowed her to continue her relationship with you. And definitely be grateful that I'm good to her."

"Good to her?" he asked with a chuckle. "Keeping her as a prisoner is your idea of being good to her."

"Trust me, it could be a lot worse." I'd seen suffering that most people couldn't imagine. I broke a man's skull with my shoe, as I'd done dozens of times before. It was my favorite way to execute my enemies. One day, that was exactly how Lucian would die.

"I guess we have different definitions of worse." Case was unusual because he wasn't afraid to challenge me, whether we were alone or in a room full of people. His bravery wasn't a façade or false display of masculinity. He was a true man down to the bone. He refused to be intimidated, but he was also highly logical, making pragmatic decisions that spared his life. He didn't want to fold when I demanded a cut of my business, but he was smart enough to understand he had no other choice. He didn't think with emotion, but reason. His sister was very similar in that regard.

"When are you going to tell her about your little operation?"

"I'm surprised you haven't told her already," he countered.

"It's not my secret to tell."

His eyes softened, just slightly.

"I'm not a rat. But you need to tell her because she'll eventually figure out that we had some kind of relationship before this came about. She's very smart...which can be fucking annoying. And I'm not a liar. If she presses me into a corner, I'm going to have to admit there's something there. Then she'll be even more pissed off when she marches to your door and discovers the horrifying truth. And trust me, she'll be horrified."

"It's not like I'm the Skull King. It's not like I'm in trafficking."

"Doesn't matter. She'll be pissed that you're involved in my world at all. She knows the kind of shit I do at night and doesn't want you to be part of that. She's not going to be happy."

"Then maybe she doesn't need to know."

I shook my head slightly. "She'll figure it out eventually. Better to come clean about it."

He tossed the towel on the counter and crossed his arms over his chest.

"She looks up to me. Don't want her to be disappointed in me."

I knew that wasn't an excuse. He was simply talking out loud, not even directing those words at me.

I didn't have anyone in my life to protect, anyone to disappoint. My only family was just as evil as I was. There was nothing I could do to change Heath's opinion of me. We've been murdering and stealing for a long time. "I have a favor to ask of you."

He lifted his gaze to meet mine. He had the exact same eyes as Cassini, so it was always jolting to meet his look. The Cardello family line was impossible to ignore. They were all strong, proud, and bossy. "What makes you think I would do anything for you?"

"Because I'm good to your sister. I bring her here because I know it's important to her. I never lay a hand on her. I never force her to do anything she doesn't want to do. Maybe I keep her as a prisoner, but I treat that woman with respect."

"Until you return her to Lucian or kill her," he said coldly.

"Let's not skip to the end."

"And let's not pretend your actions are okay just because you're decent to her now. You can say the same thing to a lamb, that the lamb should appreciate his master for being fed, for having shelter, and for having affection once in a while. None of that matters because he's going to be slaughtered—just the way my sister will be." There was so much hatred in his eyes, so much rage directed at me. If only he were powerful enough, he would actually try to kill me. Murder was written in his gaze.

"I want to know Evan's last name."

Once he heard those words, his rage turned from a boil to a simmer. "Why?"

"I'm going to kill him." I was glad Cassini was mine to enjoy. I was glad I had the perfect way to torture Lucian, the perfect leverage to get what I wanted. But I respected this woman and knew she deserved better. None of this would have happened if that piece of shit had done the right thing. He should pay for what he did.

"She doesn't want him to die."

"I don't care what she wants."

"But you're doing this for her—so you do care."

I couldn't argue with that logic. "He deserves to be punished."

"Agreed."

"So tell me."

"He's got a family."

"I'm not there for them, only him." I didn't have any interest torturing a woman and a child because of Evan's past. They probably had no idea the rotten thing that he did. They couldn't be punished for that. I hurt people who deserved to be hurt. His family didn't fall into that category. "I'll wait until they're gone. So, are you going to tell me or not?" I grew impatient, even though I wasn't going to storm off and beat him that instant. But I wanted to dig into this guy, torture Evan for what he did to Cassini. A beautiful woman like her never should have been part of the underworld. She was too good for Lucian, and she was definitely too good for me. She was an innocent person so I should let her go, but I was far too obsessed with her now. I couldn't imagine being with another woman after her. None would compare. And she was instrumental in my plans with

Lucian. Sometimes innocent people had to get hurt. If she asked me to save her in the beginning, I would have done it, even with Lucian as her husband. But that was her fault for never asking.

"Evan Alfonsi. He lives in Florence."

"Thank you."

"Cassini made us promise not to hurt him. But since you've made no such promise, give it to him good."

"Oh, I definitely will."

WE LEFT the factory and drove back to my place.

"The pasta was delicious, wasn't it?" She had an arrogant smile on her face, like she didn't need to hear my answer to know she was right.

"It was."

"Wouldn't it be nice to have that once a week for dinner? I could make it."

"Once a week is still too often."

"Are you serious? My family used to eat it every night."

"Did your family look like this?" I lifted up my shirt while I faced the road, showing my hard abs.

She glanced because she couldn't resist and then quickly looked away.

"Besides, it has no nutritional value."

"Deliciousness isn't part of that?"

I shook my head. "Sorry, baby." Not everyone could eat whatever they wanted and look sexy. This woman ate highly processed, sweet cereal and still had perfect curves. She ate donuts for lunch, lasagna for dinner, it didn't matter. Cassini could do whatever she wanted. If I ate like that, it wouldn't matter how much I worked out. I'd look like shit.

"I could never have your discipline. The doctor could tell me it would shorten my life span by ten years, and I still wouldn't stop."

"I think it would—if you had children."

She gave a slight shrug. "You and Case played nice while I was gone?"

"Did anyone die today?"

"No."

"Then yes."

She shook her head slightly. "You two are a lot alike. Maybe that's why you bump heads so much."

We were a lot alike, actually. But the real reason he despised me was because of what I did to his sister. I refused to give her up, and that just made him feel worthless. All he wanted was to protect his family, but I made that impossible. I was simply too powerful to take down. It would be a suicide mission. "Yeah...that must be it."

I pulled into the compound, and then we rode the elevator to the top floor.

"Is your brother moving out?"

"No." I shed my jacket and hung it up on the coatrack near the elevator doors.

"Why not? I don't want him barging in here if I'm watching TV on the couch in just my underwear."

"He won't."

"He already did it once."

"And he won't do it again."

She turned to me, her arms across her chest. She was

pissed she wasn't getting her way. If only she understood that I would do anything to protect her. If I really thought Heath was a threat, I would remove him.

"You have my word."

"You're really going to stick your neck out for him?" she asked. "Or are you just blinded because he's your brother."

I wasn't blinded by anything. "I understand my brother is a pain in the ass. He's more emotionally driven, less pragmatic than I am. He can be sleazy and cross the line. But I can tell you with complete confidence that he would never do anything inappropriate toward you."

"He already did—"

"It won't happen again. And nothing worse will happen. He apologized to me and seemed sincere. He said he wants to patch up things with you."

"Why would he want to do that?"

"Because if I'm not around, he is. If you need something, he can help you. If someone bothers you, he can protect you."

"He doesn't seem like the protector type."

I didn't divulge the full conversation because I didn't want her to know my brother actually thought that she meant something to me, that she was special to me. That he wanted to protect her because I valued her so much. So I left all that out. "He is. He knows you're my woman, and he wants to keep you safe. You're important to me, and therefore, you're important to him."

"I'm your woman?" she asked incredulously. "What's that supposed to mean?"

"It means what it means." I swallowed my pride at the insult in her tone.

"You mean, I'm your *prisoner*." She stepped closer to me, her heels tapping against the floor. "Big difference."

"Maybe you're my prisoner. But you're also my woman. You're the one in my bed every night. You're the one sleeping on the couch until I come home. You're the one always worried that I'm going to be in between another woman's legs. You see me as your man so let's not pretend otherwise."

She pressed her lips together tightly, having no rebuttal.

I knew I'd won that argument. "We're getting a drink at his place and watching the game tonight."

"What?"

"I spent the day with your brother. You can spend the evening with mine."

"Whoa, hold on." She raised her hand. "Are we a married couple going back and forth between families now?"

"No. I took you to see your brothers because it's important to you. Would you rather not do that anymore?"

"That's not what I said—"

"Then you're spending the evening with my brother to give him another chance."

"What if I don't want to?"

"I don't care. You're my prisoner, as you pointed out. You do as I say."

Both of her eyes heated and shot lava like two little volcanoes. "He's a creep—"

"You really think I'd let anything happen to you?"

That shut her up.

"I don't have to be in the room to keep you safe. My presence, my power, follows you everywhere you go. You're untouchable as long as you're mine. I know my brother didn't make a good first impression, but he's a good guy. He may be a criminal, but he's never forced himself on a woman or treated one with disrespect."

"And I'm just supposed to believe that?"

"Yes." I stepped closer to her. "Because I wouldn't lie to you. So we're doing this, and you're giving it your best effort."

"You seem to keep forgetting that he's the one who started all of this. He could have walked inside and introduced himself instead of saying he wanted to eat my pussy. I promise you, the conversation would have gone much differently."

"In his defense, any guy who looks at you wants to eat your pussy. So get over it."

Her hands moved to her hips. "Oh, you're definitely not getting sex tonight."

"Whatever you say, baby."

18

CASSINI

W e rode the elevator down to the third floor, and the doors opened on a floor identical to the one Balto had.

Balto stepped inside. "We're here."

It took me an extra second to step out of the elevator. I'd been mistreated to a worse degree than what Heath did to me, but I despised his deception. He'd walked in there hoping I would assume he was Balto just so he could fuck with my head. I found that cowardly. At least the other men in my life were straight about their intentions—and their identities.

Heath rose from the couch and approached us in the entryway. He wore sweatpants that hung low on his hips and a black t-shirt. His skin was blemished in certain places. It was subtle and not striking enough to notice, but now I could see all the differences between these two men. "What do you want to drink? Scotch on the rocks?"

"Always," Balto answered.

Heath looked at me, and thankfully, he didn't try to greet me with a physical gesture. "And the lady? Wine?"

"I'll have a beer."

Heath smiled in the exact same way his twin did. "You've got good taste." He walked to the bar and prepared the glasses. I was given a frosty mug for my beer, a nice and unnecessary touch. "The game is pretty boring so far. No one has scored. Cassini, do you follow football?"

"No." I answered with short words because that was all I could manage.

Balto gave me a discreet look of disapproval.

I didn't care. I didn't owe his brother anything. I hardly owed Balto anything.

We moved to the couch. I sat in the middle and Balto sat right beside me. His hand moved to my thigh and took up the entire area. It was a kind of affection he'd never showed before. He never held my hand or put his arm around my waist when we were in public. When we watched TV on the couch at home, he didn't even touch me then. The only affection I received was when we were in bed together. Maybe he only touched me now to make me more comfortable around Heath.

"How's your beer?" Heath asked. "If you don't like it, I can get you another."

"It's fine." I kept my eyes on the TV even though I wasn't following the game. My brothers were into sports, but I never was. I'd preferred helping Mom in the kitchen while they screamed at the TV.

Heath and Balto started to talk about the game like I wasn't even there. They bitched at the refs, called out the players for faking injuries, and then argued with each other about their own opinions.

The night felt awkward because the attention wasn't on me.

Balto excused himself to the restroom.

That's when things got really uncomfortable.

Heath sighed as he looked at me. "I'm sorry, alright? How many times do I have to apologize?"

"It doesn't matter how many times you apologize. Have you ever met someone and immediately didn't like them? It has nothing to do with remorse. Does it really matter if I like you or not? I'm not going to be around forever, so it really doesn't make a difference."

He held his beer between his legs and sighed to himself. "I guess I just want you to understand I would never hurt you or cross the line. I made a bad first impression, but I couldn't help it. I see a pretty girl, and all pragmatism goes out the window. But nothing else would have happened. I genuinely went up there to check on you."

"Not once did you introduce yourself."

"No, but you're a total babe, and you were wearing practically nothing. Sorry, but I'm a man. When I see a beautiful woman, I do stupid shit. I shove my foot in my mouth and act like an ass."

"You must not get laid often."

"To the contrary, actually."

"Only because you pay for it."

He chuckled. "You're witty. But no, I don't pay for sex—that often. In my experience, women like the attention."

"I'm sure they would feel differently if you just barged into their house unannounced."

"Good point. But again, I thought my brother told you I lived on the third floor. Not my problem."

I drank my beer and turned back to the TV.

"I'm cold and heartless just like my brother. We're a lot alike, and sometimes I'm worse. He's got stronger morals, stronger dedication to keeping a respectable reputation. Me...I care more about doing whatever the fuck I want."

I turned back to him, somewhat troubled by his identical features. His voice was deep like Balto's, and his jawline was so chiseled. Anytime he spoke, all the muscles in his jaw and throat shifted in the same way. Just as handsome and just as strong, this man easily could be mistaken for his brother.

"And frankly, I couldn't care less if you like me. I don't care if you respect me. Your opinion of me doesn't make me lose sleep at night. But I do want to make this right for one reason—my brother. Balto and I haven't been close for years. We butt heads a lot, and I was pretty pissed when he threw my ass in jail. We've got a lot of issues to work out. But make no mistake, he's my brother, and I would do anything for him."

His little speech started to wear me down.

"Maybe he won't admit this to you. He won't admit it to me either. But you mean something to him. He cares about you. Before he even knew about your connection to Lucian, we would go to the bars, and he wouldn't pick up anyone. When we would be at the Underground, strippers and whores would throw themselves at him, and he would say no every time. Trust me, that's not like him. He likes sex even more than I do."

So Balto really didn't want to tell me the truth the other

night. He would rather keep his silence than admit he hadn't been with anyone before he took me from Lucian. Why would he want to hide that?

"So, if you mean something to him, then you mean something to me." He pointed his thumb into his chest. "And that means I want to look out for you. Maybe when he's away, you'll feel better knowing I'm downstairs. I know you disarmed me the other night, but I'm usually a better fighter than that."

"I sure hope so."

A smile melted across his face. "I'm a decent guy. I'm not gonna say I'm a good guy because I'm not. I've killed lots of people. I've stolen from people who didn't deserve it. I like violence and bloodshed. And when I see a woman I like, I make very inappropriate comments. But you can rest assured, I mean you no harm."

I could stay angry at him, but honestly, I didn't want to be angry. He seemed genuine, and if Balto trusted him, he was probably trustworthy. There was nothing Balto hated more than when someone lied to him and made him look like a fool. His brother wasn't an exception to that. "Alright...I'll give you another chance."

"Good. But don't expect me to stop saying you're hot. Because you are damn hot."

I rolled my eyes. "Don't let Balto hear you say that."

"He doesn't care. It's the touching he cares about."

"Should we hug it out?"

He shook his head. "Definitely not. Balto explicitly told me I couldn't touch you. So clinking our beers together will have to do." He held up his glass.

I tapped mine against it.

Then we both took a long drink.

Balto came out a second later. "No guns are drawn. That's a good sign."

"We had a good talk," Heath explained. "I told her I was an asshole, but a good asshole. You know, the kind that might compliment your ass in a short dress, but not the kind that would actually keep you as a prisoner."

"Was that a dig at me?" Balto returned to the seat beside me.

"Do you know anyone else who keeps a woman as a prisoner?"

"A lot, actually," Balto replied.

"Well, yes, that was a dig at you." Heath looked at me. "So I shouldn't be the one you need to worry about. I don't have to chain up a woman to get sex."

I didn't have to come to Balto's aid, but I did anyway. "He doesn't either."

Balto slowly turned to me, his eyes showing his approval.

Heath turned his attention to the game. "If you guys are about to do something disgusting, you should head up to your place. Because I'll probably watch and like it."

———

AFTER THE GAME WAS OVER, we headed back to the top floor. It was getting late, and I wanted to go to bed at a reasonable hour. Balto always kept me up late, so I woke up around noon. But we'd had a long day of running around, so I was ready to hit the sheets.

I walked into the bedroom and opened his drawer to

fish out a t-shirt. I grabbed a white one made of soft cotton. It smelled like his detergent with a hint of his cologne. I'd been wearing his clothes so much and sleeping in his bed that I constantly smelled like him—not that I minded.

"Am I still not getting sex tonight?" He leaned against the doorframe, his hands in his pockets and his piercing blue eyes glued to me. His jeans fit his narrow hips perfectly, and he had the broadest shoulders.

"Depends." I pulled off my clothes and pulled his shirt over my naked body.

"On?"

I turned around and slowly made my way toward him, my panties the only article of clothing I had on underneath. "Your brother told me when we started seeing each other, you weren't yourself. You'd go to the bars together, but you wouldn't pick up anyone. Women would offer themselves to you at the Underground, but you never took the bait. He never saw you with anyone."

Balto held my expression, wearing that classic poker face that was impossible to read. Even an expert psychologist wouldn't be able to crack his hard shell. He had the coldest look of the hardest criminals in the country. He could give nothing away better than anyone. "My brother isn't with me all the time."

"So everything he said wasn't true?" Balto claimed he never lied, so now was his chance to prove it.

His eyes shifted back and forth slightly as he looked into mine.

"Balto?"

"Yes, it's true. But we aren't together all the time. No one knows where I am all the time besides me. Don't put too much stock in what he says."

"If that's true, why did you want me to forgive him so much? If he's not credible, why do you want me to trust him?"

Balto turned silent.

I had him cornered, and he wasn't going anywhere. Balto didn't want to show his hand, but I already knew what cards he had. He kept them close to his chest, but I was yanking them down to the table.

I walked back to the bed and peeled off my thong. It slid down my long legs until it hit the rug around his bed. Then I took off the soft t-shirt I'd just put on. Buck naked, I moved onto his bed and lay on my back. I opened my legs to him and rubbed my fingers against my clit.

He stared right between my legs, his jaw tightening and the front of his jeans getting noticeably tight. When he couldn't resist the temptation, he came toward the bed and pulled his shirt over his head. His jeans came next, along with his boxers. When his enormous cock was revealed, it was long, thick, and ready to blow.

"Were you with anyone else before you took me?"

He got onto the bed and moved to his knees. "What does it matter?"

"It matters because I think it matters." I pressed my foot against his chest to keep him in place. My fingers kept rubbing my clit, coating my entrance with slickness. My nipples were hard, and my breathing was deep and erratic. "Now, answer me."

He grabbed me by the ankle and lowered my foot before he moved farther over me.

I pressed my foot against him again. "Answer me, or I'm going to make myself come and then go to sleep."

He watched my fingers work my clit as his wide chest expanded harder against my foot. He could probably see my slickness drip down toward my crack. We'd spent four nights apart, and he hadn't caught up on the time we missed.

His eyes flicked back to mine, his irritation obvious in the vein in his forehead. He was pissed I'd commandeered the power in the situation, and he was pissed he was falling right into my trap. The smart thing to do would be to walk away and leave me there, but he wanted this pussy too much. "No. There was no one else."

I finally got the answer I wanted, so I widened my legs and gave him permission to move on top of me.

His narrow hips fit right between my thighs, and he guided his shaft with his hand. He pressed his thick crown inside me and sank perfectly, sliding through my wetness until he was buried to the hilt. "Fuck."

My ankles locked around his waist, and I pulled him close to me, our lips almost touching. My hand glided up his strong chest, and I looked into those blue eyes that always bored into mine when I came. "I already knew the answer. I just wanted to hear you say it."

19

BALTO

She lay there half asleep, satisfied by my deep thrusts and the pile of come sitting inside her. Her hair was a mess from the way I'd fisted it like a rope, and she looked so beautiful with those plump lips that had been thoroughly kissed.

I slipped out of bed and started to get dressed.

When she heard the sound of my movements, she sat up in bed and looked at me, her eyes heavy because of her desire to sleep. She watched me pull on my jeans. "You aren't leaving tonight, are you?"

"I've got a lot of work to do, baby."

"But you were gone for four nights just days ago."

"That was all your doing." I pulled on my t-shirt then ran my fingers through my short hair. My boots came on next.

She slipped out of bed and pulled on one of my t-shirts, pouting in disappointment. "When will you be home?"

"When I get home."

"Balto—"

"I'm not being a smartass. I never know what the night holds. Maybe I'll be back in a few hours. Maybe I won't come back at all." I didn't want Cassini to get the wrong impression about the two of us. Heath threw me under the bus, and now this woman assumed my monogamy meant something. It didn't mean a damn thing. Nothing had changed between us. She was the prisoner, and I was the captor. She was a key component in this war with Lucian, and I would use her in whatever way was necessary. These domestic conversations about when I'd be home were irritating.

"Don't say things like that," she whispered.

"Isn't that exactly what you want? For me to die so you can be free?" I turned to her to see her reaction, to see the emotions dancing across her face.

"I definitely want to be free. But no, I don't want you to die." She left the bedroom and walked to the living room.

I followed behind her and slipped a pistol into the back of my jeans. My beat-up truck was packed with shotguns and weapons that were practically hidden in plain sight. If someone tried to fuck with me, they were dealing with an armory.

With arms crossed over her chest and that same irritation in her eyes, she looked pissed that I was leaving. "Will Heath be downstairs?"

"No. He'll be at the Underground with me."

"Oh…"

"But there are fifty highly trained men down there. I don't know how many times I have to say it, but they'll keep you safe."

"Balto, it doesn't matter how strong they are. They aren't

you." She hit the button on the wall so the elevator would rise to our floor. "I guess I'll see you sometime in the morning." She rose on her tiptoes so she could plant her hands on my chest and kiss me.

Kiss me like she would actually miss me.

Kiss me like I meant something to her.

My hands moved around her waist, and I pulled the t-shirt tight against her body. I could feel the steep curve in her back, the prominent feminine features that made her so perfect. She had a tight back that led to a gorgeous, nectarine ass. I pulled her against my chest as I kissed her, realizing I was kissing a woman goodbye, something I'd never done before. I hardly kissed women at all. When it came to sex with whores, it was right down to business. With one-night stands, sometimes there was lip-locking but not much.

But I seemed to kiss this woman every single day.

THE SECOND I walked into the Underground, Brutus came to my side. "Hunter's replacement just delivered his fee. Not only did he pay his portion for the last distribution, but he made up for all the payments Hunter missed."

I moved past the other men and headed to the bar. "I like this guy."

"He's a good replacement."

"Should have been him in the first place. Looks like we won't have any problems from here on out."

"Not if he wants to keep his skull intact."

I stopped when I noticed Heath sitting at one of the

tables with the topless bartender in his lap. His glass of scotch was beside him, and he was feeling her up underneath her skirt. She had men to serve and tables to wait on, but my brother's mind immediately went to pussy. "We'll talk later." I left Brutus and interrupted my brother's playtime. "Let the woman do her job, Heath."

"Come on, she deserves a break." He gripped her thigh and kissed her neck.

I didn't want to sit there and watch soft porn. "Denise, get me a scotch on the rocks—now."

She was a sassy woman, but she didn't question my tone. She left Heath's lap immediately and headed back to the bar.

Wise decision. I would have fired her ass if she disobeyed me.

"What the hell, man?" Heath rounded on me. "Don't cockblock me."

"Bartenders are off-limits. You know that."

"Why the fuck are they off-limits?" He glanced at her before he turned back to me. "She's wearing a tight little skirt while her tits hang out. You expect a bunch of Skull Kings to behave ourselves around tits and booze?"

"You can fuck her after her shift but not during. If she's grinding against your dick, then our mouths are going dry. Consider this to be your one and only warning." My brother's personality was really blossoming now that he'd been out of jail for over a month. He'd shed his hard, outer layer and finally returned to the pain in the ass he used to be. I was happy for him, but he had to obey me. This was my joint, and I couldn't give him special treatment. The respect of my men was worth everything to me. Once you lost it, it was gone forever.

Denise returned and set the glass of booze beside me. "Anything else, Balto?"

With my elbows resting on the table, I looked up to meet her gaze. "Yes. Stop fucking around, or find a new job."

She didn't talk back to me or give me attitude. I was so used to Cassini always giving me hell for everything that I expected Denise to do the same thing. Instead, she held her tongue and walked away.

Heath gave me a cold look but didn't say anything.

"There's plenty of pussy out there, Heath. You'll be fine."

He grabbed his glass and took a long drink. "We've got some big players coming to the auction tonight. But I guess they're expecting younger meat."

Some of our clients preferred the women to be under eighteen, but I'd banned that months ago. That shit didn't sit right with me, and I didn't care how our clients felt about it. "Not gonna happen." I was a man with no morals and there wasn't a line I was afraid to cross, but auctioning off underage women was simply disgusting. I dealt with the cruelest men in this world, but I didn't want to make deals with those particular kinds of men.

"They'll be disappointed."

"You think I give a damn?" I wasn't even sure why we still had the auction. We made money in many other ways, and in my eyes, more respectable ways. Money was made by selling products, whether that was drugs or weapons. Sometimes we killed for a paycheck. But selling a human being into slavery seemed pathetic. Though, the auction had been around for so long that it was part of our brand. If I tried to get rid of it, the men would be angry.

"Just letting you know." He raised both his hands in the air.

I felt a pair of eyes settle on my face from across the room. It was a sixth sense, detecting someone's focus on you. I lifted my gaze and met the stare of a Skull King I could hardly tolerate. Vox, a large man who had a muscularity that could rival my own. With a black beard and matching eyes, he had the look of the devil. He was quiet, choosing to have his conversations with just his eyes. He was a strong man and one of my best fighters, but it was obvious he despised me. If he had it his way, he would be the new Skull King. He had his own supporters—but I had far more.

"What?" Heath asked, recognizing my distraction.

"Nothing." I broke eye contact with Vox, not because I backed down, but because I had more important things to worry about. "Why did you tell Cassini all that bullshit?" My fingers wrapped around my glass as I stared at my brother.

"What bullshit?"

"Don't play dumb with me. You're too dumb to pull it off."

"What?" he asked. "About you keeping your dick in your pants?"

"Exactly that, asshole."

"Well, it's true."

"But why did she need to know that?"

"Because she didn't understand why I cared so much

about us having a clean slate. So I told her she obviously meant something to you."

My fingers squeezed the glass, and I almost shattered it. The only reason I didn't was because I restrained myself, stopping my hard fingers from exerting the pressure that would make all the individual shards break apart. "Why the fuck would you tell her that?"

"Because it's the truth."

"It's not the goddamn truth. That woman is a damn poker chip. She's my ticket to taking down Lucian. Don't put false bullshit in her head to make her think she's actually got a chance of survival. She's just livestock. I'll either sell her, keep her, or butcher her. Those are her only three options."

"Balto, I could tell her all kinds of bullshit, and she would never believe it. The reason why she believes this is because she's seen it with her own eyes. If I told her you were a father of three and had a wife somewhere, you think she'd believe me? No. If I told her you were actually a woman, you think she'd believe me? No. She believes this because she already suspected it. So get angry at me all you want, but this is entirely your fault." He poked his finger into my arm. "And what's so bad about actually caring about this woman? She's beautiful, smart, has an attitude full of venom."

"I don't want to mislead her."

"How?"

"I don't want her to think I won't betray her. Because I will." I grabbed my glass and took a drink. "Even if I do care about her, if Lucian gives me what I want, I'll give her up. She needs to understand I'm still her enemy. She needs to understand she's not safe. I don't lie to my victims and let them believe they've been rescued when they've actually been kidnapped. Not my style. So don't poison her mind with this bullshit."

"If all that is true, then I'm not the one poisoning her. You are." He took a drink. "You're the one sweeping her off her feet. If you want her to understand how evil you are, then you need to start acting like it. Because all I see is a man so deep inside one pussy that he'll never get out... because he doesn't want to get out."

I sat on my throne and stared at the men sitting at the tables in the dark. Most of them were in suits, sitting alone with their paddles on the table beside them. All from different places with different backgrounds, they were men with one thing in common.

They were pigs.

The auction hosted by the Skull Kings kept our contacts fresh. It usually opened new lines of business with powerful players. They were there to buy a woman, but they also might commission us for another line of work.

I drank from my glass and watched the frightened women line up on the stage, all naked and in chains.

Call me old-fashioned, but a real man shouldn't have to force a woman to get laid. He could land pussy on his own, or he had a wallet fat enough to pay for it. Buying a slave to rape and torture was reprehensible.

It would be easy to call me hypocritical, but I certainly didn't force Cassini to do anything. It seemed like she wanted me more than I wanted her sometimes, even though that was hard to believe.

Vox came from my right, heading toward me with that scowl he always wore. That was the expression he constantly held, but it seemed more pronounced when he looked at me. He approached my throne and addressed me with his silence.

"Yes?" I asked, annoyed that I had to interact with this asshole at all. Sometimes I considered killing him because I knew what kind of ambitions he had, but that would be unfair. I would be killing him just to get him out of the way, and that wasn't justice, especially when he was a good soldier and excellent torturer.

"Our clients are complaining."

"About?" The stage was lined with beautiful women, and their glasses were full. What the hell was there to complain about?

He stood at the foot of my throne, his eyes blacker than the sky on a moonless night. "They say we don't have young women anymore."

"These women are young." They were all in their twenties. And younger wasn't necessarily better, in my opinion.

"Not young enough. We're going to lose our best clients if we—"

"The answer is no. They can deal with it or go elsewhere."

His arms stayed by his sides, but his annoyance was obvious in the tightness of his limbs. There was noticeable distance between us, but the proximity was enough to be hostile. "If the Skull Kings fail to do the cruel things we're known for, people will lose respect—"

"We do plenty of cruel things. But we don't do that."
Criminals prided themselves on the horrors they committed. But at a certain point, some crimes were too horrific to
be proud of. Selling underage women was repulsive. That
didn't make us more admirable. It made us more pathetic.
"That's final. Ask me again and see what happens." I held
his gaze with my drink in my hand, prepared to crush his
skull with the tumbler if I had to.

Vox stared me down with equal intensity, wanting to
challenge me but being too smart to actually do it. He gave
a slight nod then stepped away, backing down because I
was a king you didn't want to cross.

I watched him walk away then turned my attention to
the stage as the auction began.

20

BALTO

H eath and I sat at the curb in the truck outside the apartment building. It was seven in the morning, the time of day when everyone left for work.

He ran his fingers through his hair as he released a loud yawn. "What the hell are we doing, Balto? You've got a beautiful woman waiting for you, so why are we parked at a random curb?"

"There's someone I want to see." I looked out my side window and stared at the apartment building. On the second floor lived a family I was particularly interested in. My eyes stayed on the lobby door, and I waited for something to happen.

"Who?"

"I'll show you in a second."

Heath pulled up the sleeve of his jacket and looked at his watch. "I should be sleeping or fucking right now."

"You can do that when we're done."

Heath slumped in the seat and closed his eyes. "I never should have gotten into this truck with you."

"I never should have let you live with me."

"Come on, I'm a pleasant neighbor."

"Pleasant isn't the right word." My truck was ordinary, so it never attracted attention. If I drove everywhere in a million-euro car, people would notice me right away. And not only would they notice me, but they would remember me.

After minutes of silence, Heath spoke. "You and Vox got bad blood."

"Something like that..."

"What's his beef?"

"He wants the throne." He wants the chair that overlooks the rest of the men. He wants the power to give the orders. He wants the authority to sell young women into slavery.

"Then why hasn't he challenged you?"

My elbow rested on the inside of the door as my fingers relaxed against my lips. My eyes kept waiting for the man to appear, the man I wanted to strangle until he turned black and blue. The only reason murder wasn't on the menu was because Cassini didn't want that. If it were entirely up to me, this would have a very different outcome. "One, he couldn't defeat me. And two, I have more support. The men don't want a replacement in leadership. Vox would just alienate himself and turn everyone against him."

"If he's that ambitious, he'll challenge you eventually."

I shrugged. "Maybe."

"So, who we are stalking right now?" He turned his gaze out my window.

At that exact moment, the object of my bloodlust appeared. Dressed in a dress shirt and tie, he stepped out of the lobby doors and down the concrete stairs. In slacks and a fancy watch, he looked like a banker and or an accountant. He had classic good looks, a nice jawline, and pretty eyes. A wedding ring sat on his left hand.

I despised this man more than all my enemies.

"Is that who you were waiting for?" Heath asked, picking up on my intensity.

"Yes." I watched him walk to his car on the sidewalk and get inside. He started the engine then drove away. I stared him down as he passed, but he was so oblivious, he didn't even notice the threat in my eyes.

"And who is he? Seems harmless."

He was harmless to me, but not to the woman in my bed. He'd hurt her beyond repair, sentenced her to a life she didn't deserve. The man deserved payback far worse. "His name is Evan Alfonsi."

"Is that name supposed to mean something to me?"

I started the engine and turned my gaze on my brother. "He's the asshole Cassini sacrificed herself for. She married Lucian to spare his life, and now he's married with a kid. But he only waited three months before he tied the knot."

Understanding slowly moved into his gaze. "And now it's time to even the scales?"

I nodded. "I'm not letting him get away with that."

My brother stared at me for a long time, like he wanted to say something but thought better of it.

I could read his mind. "I respect this woman. She's had to live a terrible life, all because of him. I'll never let her go, but that doesn't mean I don't think she deserves better. She deserves a lot better."

"So you're going to kill this guy?"

"No." I hit the gas and pulled onto the road. "Just make him shit his pants a bit."

EVAN WAS a loan officer at a bank. He had a private office in the back of the hallway, which made it the perfect location to catch him off guard. Heath and I sat in the lobby until our names were called, like two regular people looking to get a loan.

We moved down the hallway.

"What's the plan?" Heath asked under his breath.

"There is no plan." I stepped inside the office and found Evan sitting behind his desk. Now that I was up close and in the same room, I took in his features, failing to understand why Cassini thought she'd loved this man at one point. What was there to love? He might be handsome, but he wasn't built the way I was. He didn't have that confidence in his gaze that I possessed. I doubted he could fuck as well as I could.

He finished typing his email before he rose to his feet. "I'm Evan, the chief loan officer here. Nice to meet you both." He extended his hand to shake mine.

I ignored it and took a seat in the leather armchair.

Heath did the same.

When Evan realized my dismissal was intentional, he slowly lowered his hand and took a seat. "Alright...how can I help you?" He smoothed the front of his tie down his chest as he sank into the leather chair. His upbeat demeanor dissipated in light of our coldness.

My hands rested on the armrests of the chair, and my fingers slowly drummed against the leather. This man wasn't worthy of Cassini. Ordinary and boring, he had nothing special about him. I shouldn't be surprised that he hadn't had the balls to defend her from Lucian. "Cassini Cardello. That's what you can help me with."

That caught him off guard visibly because his entire body tightened at the name. He slowly leaned back against his chair, distressed at the mention of his old lover, the lover he betrayed. He glanced at my brother then again at me, sizing up his two opponents.

We both knew he didn't stand a chance.

Evan stayed silent, probably because anything he said in that moment would only hurt him.

I said nothing because the silence was powerful enough to unnerve him.

Heath turned to me. "Should we check his underwear? Looks like he shit himself."

Evan's eyes shifted back and forth between the two of us. "Leave before I call the cops."

The pathetic threat was so sad, I couldn't stop myself from laughing. "A real man makes his own threats. He doesn't run to the police for protection. He protects himself. I have no idea what the hell Cassini saw in you. You're a fucking pussy."

Evan grabbed the phone and made the call.

I smiled. "This is just sad."

Evan spoke into the phone. "I've got two men in my

office threatening me." He started to describe me. "Tall, brown hair—"

"My name is Balto." Might as well speed up the process.

Heath grinned, finding the whole thing funny.

Evan repeated it over the line. "He goes by the name of Balto. He has a twin—" His eyes fell when the line went dead. "Hello?" He kept the phone to his ear even though he knew they were long gone.

"I own the police." My hands came together at chest level. "I own this city. Now I'm about to own you."

Evan slowly returned the phone to the receiver, his hand shaking slightly.

"If he didn't shit his pants before, he definitely did now," Heath said. "Look at him...he's about to faint."

The fear in Evan's eyes was nothing compared to the suffering Cassini had experienced. She became the slave and wife to a despicable man. Every day she was reminded of the freedom she gave up—for this asshole.

Evan managed to keep his voice steady enough to speak. "What do you want?"

I opened my arms, indicating to him. "This." I wanted his fear, his terror. Just as Cassini felt helpless, now so did he. There was no one he could turn to for help. I could shoot him right between the eyes without consequence. "Cassini is my woman, and as her man, it's my job to torture the people who've wronged her. That starts with you."

His chest rose and fell with his labored breaths as the fear burned in his veins. He sat across from a dangerous man he had no chance of defeating. All he could do was wait for my execution.

"Why did you do it? That woman is perfect from head

to toe. I would assume you're gay, but you married someone else three months after Cassini took your place. So explain that to me." Why would any man do something like that? I would take her place in a heartbeat, and I didn't even love her. I would never let anything like that happen to her. "What did Lucian have on you?" Evan didn't seem like he lived in the same world Lucian and I did. He worked at a bank, so he wasn't a rich tyrant. He was just an average man. So why was he mixed up with a crime lord?

Evan sighed but didn't answer.

"I suggest you cooperate," I threatened. "It'll be a lot more painful if you don't."

Evan dropped his gaze, distressed by the interrogation.

A gun could be pointed right between my eyes, and I still wouldn't flinch. A real man never showed fear, especially when it could be their last moment on this earth. That was when bravery mattered most, when terror tested your dignity. I was disappointed that this man was so weak, that Cassini actually thought she loved him at one point. No, a woman like her could never love a man as pathetic as this. "What did Lucian have on you?" Cassini never told me why Evan was in that position in the first place. It was a huge mystery.

Evan sighed again in defeat. "Don't hurt my family."

"Cooperate and I won't." I wasn't going to do it anyway, but he didn't need to know that.

"You give me your word?"

I grinned. "What makes you think my word is worth anything?"

Terror entered his gaze.

"Lucky for you, I am a man of my word," I said. "And I

won't hurt your son or your wife. But when this conversation is over, I will hurt you. There's no getting around that. You subjected Cassini to a life of servitude and torture. You'll pay the price for that."

"Don't kill me," Evan whispered. "My son needs a father." Talking about his little boy brought a thin film of moisture to his eyes.

I didn't feel bad for him. "I won't kill you. But I'll definitely hurt you. Now tell me what I want to know."

Evan was quiet for a while, probably accepting the fact that his family would be safe. But he knew terrible things would happen to him soon enough. "Lucian didn't have anything on me. He saw me with her, wanted her for himself, and made me a deal."

My eyes narrowed as the rage pumped in my veins. This wasn't a story I expected, an explanation that justified Cassini's treatment. It was a twist I'd never anticipated. "Then what happened?"

"He offered me a lot of money to go along with his plan." He could hardly meet my gaze as he spoke. "It would be the only way to get Cassini to submit, to be the prisoner he wanted. He'd been watching her for a long time, had become obsessed with her, knew exactly how she would behave if he just took her. So he had to make her do it on her terms...which is why he staged the whole thing."

I stared at him blankly as the heartbreak hit me right in the chest. Cassini had been tricked, had been manipulated into being a cooperative prisoner. I wasn't sure who I was angrier at, Lucian or Evan. "How much did he pay you?"

"A hundred thousand euros."

I closed my eyes for a moment, furious at the number.

"And you really thought Cassini was worth that meager amount? That woman is fucking priceless, but you sold her for pennies."

"Lucian said he would kill me if I didn't cooperate," Evan explained. "So I might as well take the money."

Heath shook his head. "We should kill you. A piece of shit like you doesn't deserve to live."

"No, he doesn't," I said in agreement. "You don't deserve to have a dick between your legs because you aren't a man. You never deserved to touch her or kiss her. You don't even deserve to breathe."

He bowed his head. "I did love her—"

"Say that again, and I'll shoot you between the eyes." I pulled my pistol from the back of my jeans and set it on the table beside me. It was fully loaded, and I had perfect aim. I would spray the back wall with his brains.

Evan couldn't take his eyes off the gun. "I've told you what you wanted to know. What more do you want from me?"

I wanted to murder him and Lucian at the same time, bury them deep in the soil and piss on their graves. I always described Lucian as being a pussy and an idiot, but he'd expertly trapped Cassini, making her think her actions were heroic. That was how he got between her legs, how he got a dutiful wife. Because he made up the whole fucking thing. "And you just moved on and never looked back?"

He could barely look me in the eye. "What else was I supposed to do?"

"Be a man," I said coldly. "And die for your woman. That's what men do. That's what we were put on this earth to do." I rose to my feet and grabbed my gun. "The only reason you're alive is because Cassini wouldn't want me to kill you. Consider yourself lucky."

"Does she know about all of this?" he asked.

"No." I approached his desk as I shoved the gun into the back of my jeans. "I'll be waiting for you when you get off work."

Evan glanced at the frame on his desk, a picture of his wife and young son. He turned back to me, pathetically apologetic. "And what are you going to do to me?"

I planted both hands on the desk and leaned forward. "I'm gonna take you out to the middle of nowhere and push you to the brink of death. You'll fear death in the beginning, but once the agony kicks in, you'll wish it would take you away. And that's when I'll leave you...when you beg me to finish the job."

———

WE PARKED IN THE COMPOUND, and I killed the engine.

"Are you going to tell her?" Heath asked from his side of the truck.

I'd never intended to tell her about my vendetta against Evan, but he'd told a secret that completely changed the past. Did Cassini have the right to know what really happened? Or would it only hurt her more? "I don't know."

"Knowing he'll get a beating of a lifetime later might give her closure."

Knowing her, it wouldn't. "She's too classy for that. She wouldn't want me to do it."

"Then why are you going to do it?"

"For myself. I'm the Skull King—and it's my job to pursue justice."

It was almost eleven in the morning, so the sun was high in the sky. Heath wore sunglasses on the bridge of his nose to keep the brightness out of his gaze. Winter had nearly arrived, but cloudless days like this made it feel like summer. "And what about Lucian?"

"He'll pay." He'd pay for a lot of things. I already got some vengeance when he realized I'd been screwing his wife right under his nose. She was mine long before I took her. Every time he was away on the weekend, I was buried deep inside her, making her come like he never did. "He knows about our affair."

"He does? When did he tell you that?"

"About a week ago. Cassini left her phone behind, and he went through the messages."

The corner of his mouth rose in a smile. "Talk about a declaration of war...."

"Yeah, he was pissed. But I like it when my enemies are pissed. Means I'm doing something right."

"Then you're definitely doing a lot right."

We got out of the truck and made it to the elevator.

"Want me to help you tonight?" Heath asked as we rose to his floor.

"No. That asshole is all mine."

The doors opened, and Heath stepped into his entryway. "Alright, I'm going to bed. Have fun with Evan."

"I will." The doors shut, and I rose to the top floor. Cassini wasn't on the couch where she usually was, and that was probably because of how late it was. It was nearly noon, and I was usually home by four in the morning.

Cassini stepped out of the hallway, her hair and makeup done, but she was wearing my boxers and t-shirt. "You were gone for a long time." With accusation in her eyes and an attitude in her hips, she didn't look happy to see me.

"I had a lot of work to do."

"What kind of work?"

"Ruling, collecting, threatening, torturing...the list goes on." My hand moved to her neck, and I examined her prettiness, the plumpness of her lips, and the beautiful color of her eyes. Evan betrayed her for a pathetic sum of money and married a woman who couldn't compare. The man was twisted in the head. "Miss me?"

"I'm too annoyed to miss you."

"Annoyed?"

"You were gone for nearly sixteen hours."

"That's the job, baby."

She rolled her eyes. "Well, I don't like your job."

"You'd better get used to it. It's not going to change."

"Don't expect me to change either." She stepped away from my grasp so my fingertips slid past the softness of her neck.

"Did you sleep well?" When she turned around, I stared at the way her boxers hugged her perfect ass.

"What do you think?" She walked into the kitchen and grabbed a beer.

"You want to come with me to the Underground, then?"

"Probably not." She came back, her lips sealed around the bottle.

It seemed like every time I came home from a long night, we had this same conversation again. She didn't like it when I was gone, and she was always suspicious of my activities. As the Skull King, there wasn't anything to be suspicious about. I was committing heinous crimes all night long. "You're welcome to join me whenever you want."

She continued to drink her beer, her affection nonexistent. She was clingy with me before I left, and now she was pissed at me all over again. A sassy woman with an attitude was rarely happy for long. "And do what, exactly?"

"Sit on my lap."

She made an irritated face. "Like a dog?"

"No. Like my woman." I had a long night, and I'd been looking forward to sleep, but now that this woman was in front of me, wearing my clothes with her hair styled, all I wanted to do was be buried inside her. I wanted to erase the memory of Evan, a man who never deserved to be there in the first place. I wanted to replace Lucian, to erase whatever hold he thought he had on my woman. I wanted to unshackle the invisible chains that kept her tied to the two men.

I pulled the beer from her hand and set it on the table against the wall. Then I backed her up into the dining table, making her move in reverse until her ass tapped against the corner. My shirt was yanked over my head, and my jeans were discarded.

She still seemed angry with me, but her body was responding to mine. Her fingers pushed down her boxers and panties until they slid to her ankles. She left her camisole on, but the sheer material barely covered anything anyway.

I scooped her onto the table then placed my heavy body

on top of hers. My hips maneuvered between her legs and I positioned her to take me, to have all of me. It disgusted me that a man had had this woman's heart, but he tossed it aside for money. It enraged me more that a man used her good heart against her to make her submissive. I wasn't much better than the two men, but I somehow felt entitled to have her.

I felt entitled to own her.

Once I was inside her, she gasped against my mouth.

She was slick and warm, her body indicating she wasn't the least bit angry with me.

Her fingers dug into my hair, and her lips shivered against mine. "I missed you…"

I didn't need to hear her confession to know how she felt. She was pissed the second I walked in the door, but that meant nothing. This woman could be livid, but that didn't change the fact that she wanted me, that she wanted me to be home with her, to fuck her and protect her. "I missed you too, baby."

21

CASSINI

It'd been nearly two months since I came to live with the Skull King. I'd never seen him crush a skull with my own eyes, but I knew he was capable of it. I hadn't witnessed his violence firsthand, but I knew that was what he did every night. I went from one master to another, but living with Balto had started to feel like home.

I wasn't sure what this relationship had turned into.

I'd never stayed awake during the night and waited for Lucian to come home. Instead of hoping he would walk in the door in one piece, I hoped he wouldn't walk through the door at all. But with Balto, I counted down the minutes until I knew he was safe. My imagination ran wild, and I pictured him surrounded by beautiful women, women who wanted to screw him for free.

I never cared what Lucian did behind my back.

The lines had become so blurred that I had no idea what I was doing.

Was I going to live here indefinitely?

Or was Balto going to give me back to Lucian once his demands were met?

Would he really do that to me?

Balto stepped out of the elevator at seven in the evening. He'd said he had to take care of a quick errand, but it still took him two hours. Drops of blood were on his gray t-shirt, and judging by the way it had sprayed against his clothes, it seemed like it belonged to someone else.

"Torture someone?" I stood at the kitchen counter and strained the pasta. I wasn't a big cook, but since Balto only made boring meals, I had to cook for myself if I wanted anything decent. I pressed the excess liquid out of the noodles then tossed them with the sauce—the Cardello sauce.

"Yes." Like that was a normal answer to give, he walked by and headed down the hallway. He hopped in the shower, and by the time he returned, I'd already finished my dinner.

I sat at the kitchen table and stared at my empty plate. Only streaks of sauce were left.

Balto returned, in just his sweatpants. His hard body was on display like a work of art. If he just killed someone, he didn't seem affected by the murder. Like nothing happened at all, he walked into the kitchen, whipped up something, and then took the seat across from me.

"What did he do?"

He chewed slowly as he stared at me, silently asking me to elaborate.

"The man you killed."

"I didn't kill him."

"Then what did you do?"

"Made him wish I killed him." He took another bite, his masculine jaw working slowly. He made eating fish somehow sexy, all because of that hard jawline.

"What did he do?"

He stabbed his asparagus with a fork. "Betrayed someone I know."

"You exact revenge for other people?"

"Rarely."

"Then this person must mean a lot to you."

He lowered his fork as he finished chewing, his gaze focusing even harder on my face. He said nothing, letting the silence fill the room with even more tension.

I was used to this palpable focus, when he made the entire world go quiet because he was locked on to his target with such enthusiasm, but I was never comfortable with it. It always made me feel like prey—and he was the predator. That was the status of our relationship. We weren't man and woman. We weren't man and lover. We were predator and prey. "I've been here for a while, and I've behaved. It's time you upheld your end of the bargain."

"And what is that, exactly?" He finished his food and pushed the plate to the side. His elbows rested on the surface, and he leaned toward me, his piercing blue gaze drilling holes into my skin.

"You said you would give me my freedom." I wanted to go shopping, visit my family, take a drive through the countryside. I just wanted to have some control over my life. "I haven't felt the sun on my face since I came here. At least with Lucian, I could go outside and sit by the pool."

"Don't compare me to him."

"I'm not. I'm just saying—"

"Would you rather go back to him?"

"No, but I—"

"Then don't compare me to him." He grabbed his glass of booze and took a drink.

"You said you would give me my freedom. Are you a man of your word or not?"

He shook the cubes in his glass before he set it down. "Always."

"Then I want to leave. Either give me a car, or I'll walk everywhere."

He chuckled like the suggestion was stupid. "Not gonna happen. You think I'm gonna let you walk around by yourself in this city?"

"I've been doing it my whole life."

"That was before you got yourself mixed up with two crime lords. All those freedoms you used to enjoy are long gone. You will always look over your shoulder as long as Lucian and I are alive."

Balto wasn't the one I was afraid of. I never had to look over my shoulder because it didn't matter if he was there or not. "I fuck you every night when you come home. I've made an effort with your brother. It's your turn to uphold your end of the bargain."

That amused smile spread across his mouth. "Let's not pretend you fuck me out of obligation. You fuck me because you want me. Let's start there."

Whenever he was a pompous asshole, I wanted to smack him upside the head. I wanted to do that now, but when he stared at me like that, I felt immobile. "Doesn't matter. We made a deal. Are you going to honor that deal or not?"

He rested back against the chair while his fingers held on to his glass. With his head slightly tilted, he looked at me long and hard, like he was considering his final answer before he gave it. "No."

I'd been expecting a different answer, so I couldn't swallow my shock. "No? Are you serious?"

"Dead serious."

I leaned over the table, ready to slap my palm against his face. "You said—"

"I know what I said." He slammed his glass down on the table. "But there's shit you don't know, alright?"

"Shit I don't know?" I asked blankly. "What does that mean?"

He spilled some of his booze across the wood and didn't bother cleaning it up. He took a drink before he looked at me again, his eyes filled with irritation. "Lucian called me a week ago. He went through your phone and discovered our affair."

The air left my lungs as I let out a quiet gasp. When I'd left the house, I didn't grab a single item. Everything was left behind, including my two phones. I hadn't given it a single thought since I left.

"Wasn't happy about it."

"I bet..."

Balto showed a small smile. "His pride was wounded. He was embarrassed. And then he threatened me...which was funny."

"Threatened you how?"

"Said he wouldn't negotiate with me. Said he would never give up the diamond and his intentions for you. Instead, he claims he's going to take you."

My heart started to race. I felt perfectly safe with Balto, but I didn't underestimate Lucian either.

"Which is why I have to deny you your freedom. I'm not afraid of Lucian, but I'm not careless either."

I never wanted to be with Lucian again. I never wanted to be that asshole's plaything. I was Balto's prisoner, but I felt more respected than I ever did with Lucian. I'd rather die than go back to him. "But I can't stay locked up here forever."

"I said I would take you to visit your brothers."

"I need more than that. I want to go out to dinner, go shopping, just get out of the house..."

He gave me that unreadable expression.

"I've got cabin fever over here. I just can't keep staying in the house all the time."

"What do you want me to do?" he asked in a bored voice. "Take you out to dinner?"

"Yes."

His eyes narrowed in surprise.

"If I can't go out by myself, then you need to take me places. I feel like an unwanted dog trapped in here."

He stared at me for a long time as he considered it.

"Consider it a compromise. It's too dangerous for me to go out alone. But I can go out with you." Lucian was far more likely to snatch me if I was unprotected. I saw first-hand how scared Lucian was of Balto. That gave me a big advantage.

"I'm surprised you would risk it at all."

"Well, staying here indefinitely isn't the solution. And I know I'll be safe with you."

Balto stared at me for a long time, his eyes slowly softening.

"You really think he'll try to take me?"

He nodded. "He'll have his men try to take you. The pussy won't do anything himself."

That didn't surprise me. Lucian never did his dirty work.

"He's not thinking clearly right now. I humiliated him, and he's livid. Now he wants to lash out and teach me a lesson, even though he provoked this entire ordeal. He'll fail at the attempt, be humiliated once more, and then he'll play nice. He'll come back to the table as a negotiator."

"And will you negotiate with him?"

He brought the glass to his lips and took a drink. "Depends on what he has to offer."

"ARE YOU STAYING HOME TONIGHT?" It was almost nine, so if he was going to leave, he would do it soon. I sat on the couch with the blanket over my thighs while the game played on the TV.

He was still in his sweatpants, like he had no intention of going anywhere. "Yes."

Anytime I knew he was staying home with me, there was a noticeable spike of happiness in my system. It wasn't just about the protection, but the comfort. This man was beside me most nights, and it gave me the greatest sleep I'd ever known. When he was gone, I couldn't sleep at all.

He sat beside me on the couch, and he turned to look at

me once he finished the contents of his glass. "Were you like this when Lucian was gone?"

I almost rolled my eyes. "No. I was happy when he was gone."

"You never felt unsafe?"

It had been just me and his men, and his soldiers weren't entirely loyal. They didn't respect Lucian, so it's possible his men could have taken advantage of me while he was away. But I never cared about that possibility...probably because I didn't have anything to live for. "I guess it didn't matter. Nothing mattered."

"And with me, things matter?"

I shrugged when I couldn't supply a better response.

He stared at me for a while before he turned off the TV. "Let's go to bed." He left his dirty glass behind and tossed the remote on the coffee table. As he rose to his feet, the cushion sprang back in place noticeably when his weight was lifted. He rose to his full height, his back turned to me, and he was a statue with endless carvings. For a man who constantly saw battle, it was surprising that his skin was so flawless, that he didn't possess bullet wounds or scars from stabbings. He was completely untouched.

I watched him walk away before I returned to reality, before I remembered that I was alone in the living room, sitting in the dark.

I went into the bedroom and found him already sitting in bed, his back against the headboard with his large dick on display. His intentions were already clear, even before his eyes roamed over my body as I undressed.

I left my clothes on the rug then crawled into bed. "You're easy to read."

"And easy to please." He grabbed my hips and positioned me on top of him. He didn't get me wet by kissing me or playing with my clit. He got right to it, pushing his thick crown inside me and finding the holy grail of moisture. "You're always wet, aren't you?" He smiled slightly as his length moved within me, stretching my channel as he delved deeper inside.

Lucian wouldn't agree with that statement.

His hands hugged my rib cage, and his thumbs rested right below my tits. He pulled me up slightly then back down, wanting to test the friction between my legs. When I didn't bounce on his dick like I normally did, he raised an eyebrow. "What is it, baby?"

I didn't know what was going to happen with Lucian, but I knew I never wanted to return to his ownership. I didn't want to be his wife anymore. If it were possible, I would file for divorce so I wouldn't have to possess his last name on my driver's license. I wanted nothing to do with him. Balto was another extreme, the kind of man I never imagined meeting, but I preferred his company over everyone else's. "Don't give me back to him…" Maybe I was Balto's prisoner, but even if the door was unlocked and I was free to go, I wasn't certain I would leave anyway. This man never hurt me, he always pleased me, and I innately respected him.

His hands slid to my hips as he looked me in the eye.

"I don't want to go back to him. I want to stay here—with you." Balto was the only man in the world who could protect me, so if that meant staying by his side for the rest of my life, I was fine with that. I hated it when he was gone all night, but that was only because I cared about him. I was cooped up like a princess locked in a tower, but there was nowhere else I'd rather be.

He stared at me with those cold eyes, his thoughts a mystery.

"Don't give me back to him," I repeated, as if he hadn't heard me the first time.

His blue eyes gave nothing away.

"Balto?" I pressed my forehead against his and wrapped my arms around his neck.

"Baby, I don't know what I'm going to do." His arm hooked around my waist, and he rolled me to my back, staying inside through the maneuver. "I have no fucking idea what I'm going to do."

22

CASSINI

We sat in silence on the drive to the factory.

Balto and I hadn't said more than a few words to each other since last night. Wordlessly, we screwed over and over, filling the tension with ecstasy. He told me he would keep me if I made myself valuable, but I obviously hadn't done a good enough job if he still was considering handing me over.

But how could I ever be worth more than that diamond?

It was worth more than a small country.

It didn't matter how wet I was or how hard I made him come. I couldn't compete with that.

Balto parked the truck and we walked inside, still not saying a word to each other.

I moved to the back and found Case working on the books. "Do you ever do anything besides work?"

Case looked up, annoyance in his eyes but a smile on his lips. "No, unfortunately."

"You should go on a date sometime. Maybe having a

woman in your life would help you relax." I took the seat beside him and looked at the paperwork.

When Case noticed my gaze, he grabbed all the papers and shoved them into a folder. "Women are nothing but a distraction."

"From work?" I challenged. "That's exactly what you need."

Balto took a seat at the head of the table and looked around, examining his surroundings like he was always ready for something to jump out at him. He wore a dark blue shirt with black jeans, his muscled frame keeping him warm despite the chill that had settled on the city. He didn't welcome my brother with a greeting. He just sat there, like a gargoyle.

"Maybe in a few years," Case said.

"You're thirty," I reminded him. "If you wait too long, all the good girls will be taken."

"Not if I go for younger women," Case replied.

Balto wore a slight grin.

I rolled my eyes. "Case, just live a little. That's all I'm saying. So, what are you working on?"

"Just doing the books," he said. "Nothing new."

"How's business?" Since the company had been run by the Cardello family for generations, sales had always been strong. Italians respected our family lineage throughout the years of business.

Case suddenly turned quiet, looking at the folder like there was something hidden inside.

I knew my brother so well that I could spot his unease in a heartbeat. I knew when he was hiding something, because he hardly ever hid anything. "What is it?"

Balto chimed in. "Just tell her. She can handle it."

I stared at the man I was sleeping with, having no idea how he was involved in this. "Case, what's he talking about?"

Balto stared at Case, wearing that impenetrable poker face.

Case held his gaze before he lowered his chin to the table.

My eyes glanced back and forth between the two men.

"Get it over with, man." Balto grabbed the bottle of scotch in the middle of the table and poured himself a glass.

I looked at my brother, waiting for whatever secret he'd been hiding from me. "Case."

He swallowed a shot of scotch then wiped his mouth with the back of his forearm. "Alright. Dirk and I have been running a side business right in this factory."

I expected something a lot more scandalous than that. "Another business?"

Balto stared at me.

"Yeah," Case said. "It's been going on for a few months. It's had tremendous success, and we're going to keep doing it."

"Well, that's great," I said. "What's bad about that?"

"It's not the most respectable kind of business," Case said. "It's the reason Balto and I know each other."

"Okay..." I stared at Balto for a moment, seeing the same cold expression. "What kind of business are we talking here?" If Balto was involved, then I could only assume it was criminal. Case was clean-cut and smart, so I was surprised he would get involved in anything besides the family business.

"Drugs," Case answered. "Dirk does the cooking. We make an exceptional product. We sell it throughout the country. Balto found out what we were doing and threatened to kill me if I didn't pay my taxes."

Balto held up his glass before he took a drink.

Being with Balto taught me how terrible the world could be, but I never expected my brothers to be involved in something like that. "But the pasta business is already successful. Why would you risk everything to sell drugs?"

"Because it makes a lot of money," he said bluntly.

"So?" I snapped. "You already have a lot of money."

"Not like this," he countered. "We make more a month than we do in an entire year with just the pasta."

Case and Dirk both had beautiful homes in the countryside. They drove nice cars and had luxurious lives. Why would they risk that simplicity for something so dangerous? "Money is just money, Case. You can't take it with you. I suspect you'll be leaving this life sooner than expected, to top it off."

Case took another drink.

"Mother and Father would be disappointed…" They'd left their children with a viable company that would provide for them, but it wasn't enough. Case and Dirk wanted more even though they didn't need anything else.

Case sighed. "Cassini—"

"This stops now. No more, Case."

Case shook his head slightly. "There's nothing you can do—"

"You wanna bet?" I challenged. "Balto will end this if I ask him to."

"Balto?" he asked blankly. "He's the one who profits from it."

"Doesn't matter." I was so disappointed in my brother. "Stop this operation now, or I'll make Balto do it."

Balto stared at me, still giving nothing away.

"Balto can't stop me," Case argued. "And he doesn't want to stop me. There's nothing to worry about. Dirk and I know what we're doing."

"No, you have no idea what you're getting yourself into," I snapped. "I've been a prisoner to Lucian, a horrible man who does horrible things. I've been with Balto, a man who rules an underground world. He crushed a man's skull with his boot not long ago. And you want to get involved in that?"

"I'm not involved in that," my brother argued. "I make a product and I sell it. That's it."

I rolled my eyes. "If that's really how you see it, then I'm even more worried. It's not that simple. It's certainly not that easy. You're gonna get yourself killed."

"That's what Balto is for." Case stared at me, apology in his gaze. "He keeps business running smoothly. Someone steps on us, he steps in. Cassini, I get that you're upset, but this is what Dirk and I want to do."

"It's dangerous," I snapped. "What would I do if something happened to you?"

"Cassini..." He shook his head slightly. "You weren't involved in anything criminal, and you ended up as a slave to Lucian. Now you're Balto's prisoner. Life is risky no matter what we do. You're never safe. You can live in a house in the middle of nowhere and never interact with anyone, and you would still be at risk. So let this go."

I lived a normal life until Lucian. Evan got involved, and I laid down my life for his. Ever since that day, nothing had been the same. I changed handlers, but that didn't make me less of a prisoner.

Balto watched me for a long time, the sympathy in his gaze. His fingers rested around the glass as he stared at me. Wordlessly, he comforted me, told me that an argument was futile. "I take care of my men, Cassini."

"But shit happens anyway," I whispered.

"Yes," he said in agreement. "But rarely."

I didn't want to sit with my brother for another second, not when I was this irritated. After everything I'd suffered, the last thing I wanted was for my brothers to suffer in the same way, to get mixed up with the wrong people. They deserved a quiet and peaceful life making pasta. I ditched the chair and stormed out. "I'm ready to go, Balto."

Case's voice sounded from behind me. "Cassini."

Balto trailed behind me until he caught up with me. His arm circled my waist, and he pulled me close.

I pushed him away. "Don't touch me."

He grabbed me by the arm.

I twisted out of his grasp and spun his arm away. He was so easy to disarm that he must have allowed me to do it. I looked up into his face, seeing the hard lines that looked like the cliff face of a mountain. "You knew, and you didn't tell me."

"Not my secret to tell."

I yanked my arm back and slapped him across the face.

"I'm fucking you every night, and it's not your secret to tell?"

He turned with the hit and closed his eyes momentarily. When he turned back to me, his cheek had started to redden and rage had entered his gaze, but he was still as a statue, cold and devoid of emotion. "Do you want me to tell them that we were having an affair before I took you? That we were fucking for a month before I made you mine? Is that my secret to tell?"

I pulled my hand back and prepared to slap him again.

He grabbed me by the wrist and shoved me against the wall. His body crowded mine and kept me in place, pinning me against the wall in the hallway. "I gave you a freebie. But you won't get another one. Slap me and see what happens." He released my wrist and stepped back. "Men want money. They want power. They want women. All men are the same. You can be pissed at your brothers, but this is their decision. Let it go."

"No. You're going to stop them."

"I have no control over what they do."

"Yes, you do. Now make them stop."

He shook his head. "They make a great product, and they do it quickly."

My eyes narrowed to slits. "I don't care. This is my family."

"I keep all my men safe. The only thing they need to worry about is pissing me off. I'm the biggest enemy they could have."

I threw my arms down. "Do this as a favor to me. Please."

His eyes shifted back and forth as he looked into mine.

"What do you expect to happen? I tell them to stop, and they just listen? If I won't work with them, then they can just work with someone else. They become more vulnerable that way, then they're at a disadvantage. Working for me is the best thing for them. The only way to make this stop is if they abandon this business for good, and I'm telling you, that's not going to happen."

I felt so powerless. I wanted to protect my family but had no idea how to do that.

"You want to know how the real world works?"

I cocked my head to the side.

"The closer you are to danger, the safer you'll be. Because you always know exactly where the biggest threat is. If anything, your brothers are in less danger than they were before. All the big players know exactly who I am, and if they're under my reign, they're untouchable."

WHEN WE RETURNED to his building, I went into my room and got under the covers.

I couldn't believe how stupid my brothers were.

All I wanted was to get away from this lifestyle, but I was sinking deeper into it.

I hadn't been in this bed for a long time because I spent my evenings with Balto, but now, I wanted space. The two men knew each other even before I met Balto. That made me feel stupid—and clueless.

I stared at the other wall without really thinking about anything, just letting my mind wander to my childhood. Life was so much easier when my parents were around. I never needed someone to protect me, but now I needed someone who could guide my family in the right direction. My brothers were drug dealers, and I was a prisoner of a man who would hand me back to my original tormentor.

What would Lucian do once he got me back?

Would he kill me right away? Or torture me first?

The bedroom door opened behind me, but I didn't turn around to look at Balto. I just lay there, ignoring him.

His footsteps filled the bedroom as he stepped farther inside the room. He must have known I wasn't asleep because he didn't bother to be quiet. He grabbed the sheets and yanked them off me before he snatched my ankle and pulled me to the edge of the bed.

"What are you doing?" I kicked his grip away.

He grabbed my hips and pulled me to the edge of the bed before he got my jeans loose.

That was when I noticed he was naked, six-foot-three of pure skin and muscle. His dick was hard despite my melancholy, and he wanted me even if I didn't want him.

"I'm not in the mood."

He yanked my jeans off then pulled my panties free.

"I said no." I tried to kick him away.

Effortlessly, he gripped the insides of my thighs and pinned me wide apart as he entered me.

My eyes closed as I felt him sink inside me, meeting no resistance because I was somehow wet despite my rage.

He pulled me farther off the bed until he was completely sheathed. "I know my baby. When she's in a bad mood, she needs sex."

"That's not true—"

He gave me his slow and even thrusts, hitting me deep and hard every time.

The words died in my mouth, and I didn't protest again.

His arms hooked behind my knees, and he leaned over me as he pounded into me, his pretty blue eyes watching me come apart. He studied the way I bit my bottom lip with pleasure, the way my eyes fluttered when the pleasure felt so good between my legs. "I know what my baby needs. Don't worry, I'll give it to you."

23

BALTO

I spoke to Brutus over the phone. "Who is she?" I sat in the living room while the TV was on mute. Cassini was down the hallway in the bedroom, and she'd been there for almost an hour.

"They call her Miss Lightning."

I grinned. "Interesting name."

"She said she's earned it...whatever that means."

"So what does she want?"

"Wants you to meet her. She's been taking care of her girls for a long time, but lately, men have been knocking the girls around. When they get scars, they're worthless. The men aren't paying either. She's interested in protection."

"I'm not a pimp." I didn't deal with prostitution. That was beneath my interest. I preferred real crime, arms dealing and drug trafficking. I preferred wars fought over money instead of wars fought over women.

"She still wants to meet you."

"Still not interested."

"She seems pretty adamant. And she sounded like she had something good to offer."

I already had so many projects I had to attend to. I certainly didn't need another—unless it was worth my while. "I'll think about it." I hung up then searched for Cassini, unsure where she'd disappeared to. We hadn't discussed her brother's new career since I'd come into her room and chased her thoughts away, but there was no doubt it was still on her mind.

I moved into the bedroom and found her standing in a black dress. With a single strap across her shoulder and a high slit up her thigh, she was ready to hit the runway. Her hair was curled and pulled back slightly, revealing the beautiful skin of her neck and chest. Dark makeup was around her eyes, a smoky effect I found intoxicating. I looked her up and down and couldn't decide on my first move. Should I dig my hand into her hair and kiss her? Or should I yank up her dress and bend her over the bed?

She turned to look at me, several inches taller in her heels. She placed her hands on her hips and gave me a knowing look, as if she had the control in this situation— even though she was actually prey.

"You could just put on lingerie if you're trying to impress me."

"Wearing lingerie would get me kicked out of the restaurant."

"What restaurant?" I stepped closer to her, my hand wanting to reach for the zipper at the back and pull it down.

"The restaurant we're going to tonight. You're taking me out."

"I don't remember agreeing to that."

"Because I don't need you to agree. Now get dressed so we can go."

This woman had just bossed me around, and it was my job to put her in her place. But I was too amused to do that. Cassini had laid down the law—and it was sexy. "Where are we going?"

"There's this fancy Italian place I haven't been to in forever. I would really like to go there."

"Alright."

Her eyebrow rose slightly, as if she couldn't believe my cooperation.

"I'll take you to dinner. But I want you to suck me off when we get home."

She rolled her eyes. "You know I would have done that anyway."

My cock thickened inside my sweatpants. "Yes. But now, you'll make it really good."

———

I DIDN'T OWN a suit because I refused to wear one. Black tie wasn't my style. A powerful man didn't need to put on an image to be powerful. I could walk into any room buck naked, and people would recognize my authority. Only pussies wore suits.

All I had was a black blazer, so I wore that over my gray V-neck. I wore dark blue jeans and kept my gun tucked in the back of my waistband. A man like me never left the house without being armed. I also had a blade stuffed into the pocket of my jeans. But instead of using a gun or a knife, I preferred my bare fists—and my boots.

I drove to the restaurant and parked the truck along the curb. It was difficult to keep my eyes on the road when I kept glancing at her sexy legs in that black dress. In just a t-shirt and bare-faced, she looked phenomenal. But when she wore a tight dress and did her makeup like that, she was something else.

I knew she thought I looked good too—because she kept sneaking glances at me.

We entered the restaurant, and I was given a private table in the second room. I'd had a few business meetings here before, so the manager recognized me. Even men who didn't directly participate in crime were somehow connected to it. They knew exactly who the big players were—and I was the biggest player of all.

Our table had a short vase with a single red rose along with a small white candle. Classical music played overhead, and the sound of moving plates and clinking utensils filled the space. Conversations flowed from the other room, but they were muted by the distance.

I sat across from Cassini at the small table and stared at her, finding her more alluring than any other woman in the world. I paid top dollar for the most beautiful whores to warm my bed, but they didn't compare to this woman. Not even slightly.

Her green eyes were so hypnotic, especially when they lit up in ecstasy. Two ethereal orbs, they shone with their own light. They were so expressive, showing her fear, anger, and lust. She could tell me so much without even trying. I rarely looked a woman in the eye during sex because she was usually on all fours, but I preferred looking at this woman, enjoying every little reaction she had to me. It was the most erotic part about her, not her endless curves or smooth skin.

Her lips were my next obsession. So plump and full, they were made for kissing—and sucking. When she applied a coat of deep red lipstick, it only enhanced the curves of her mouth. Sometimes I couldn't decide what I wanted more—to kiss her or feel her suck my dick.

She picked up the menu and scanned the selections.

I didn't grab my menu because I was far more interested in her than food. Lucian must have spotted her somewhere and turned obsessive the way I had. He must have examined her perfect mouth and had the exact same fantasies I had. But the only way he could have this woman was through a lie.

"Should we get a bottle of wine?" she asked, still looking at the menu.

"I don't drink wine."

"Ever?" She raised an eyebrow and peered at me over her menu.

"You know I'm a liquor kind of man." I preferred all the classics, scotch, gin, and vodka.

"And I like beer and the occasional martini. But wine is the perfect pairing for Italian cuisine."

This woman was so beautiful that she could ask me for anything, and I would give it to her. She had more power than any person should, and thankfully, she wasn't aware of it. "Pick whatever you want."

"So, you'll share it with me?"

"Yes."

She looked at the wine list. "They've got a good selection of Barsetti wines. That's my favorite."

I recognized the name Barsetti, but I'd never tried the wine.

The waiter came to our table, and Cassini picked out the red wine she wanted. "Could we also have the bruschetta as an appetizer?"

She'd be eating that alone.

She ordered her entrée, and then I ordered the grilled chicken. I hardly ate out because the food was prepared with too much oil and other fattening substances. I'd made my choice a long time ago, that I would cut carbs and fats from my life so I could drink as much as I wanted. Most people needed food to survive, but I needed booze.

The waiter walked away then returned with the bottle of wine. He poured two glasses, brought the bruschetta, and then disappeared.

She brought the glass to her lips and left a distinguishable print of her mouth.

I imagined that same print on my dick.

"It's good." She placed a slice of bread on her plate and took a bite.

I didn't move because I was entranced by her, by the way her mouth moved as she chewed, by the way that black dress fit her so perfectly. Her olive skin was flawless, having its own distinct shine. The hollow of her throat was kissable. I could picture my tongue tasting her as my dick was buried deep inside her. My mouth craved to kiss her everywhere, going all the way around her mouth, pussy, and ass. I was a sexual man with exceptional needs, but this woman amplified my desires. Watching her do something so simple, like drink a glass of wine, was practically pornographic to me.

She finished her bruschetta. "Are you going to try one?"

I'd rather try her. "No." I grabbed the glass of wine and took a drink. If I weren't so adamant that I didn't want anyone else looking at her, I would lift her onto the table and fuck her right in the middle of the restaurant. I suspected we wouldn't make it back to the compound because I'd pull over and fuck her in the truck.

She took another piece and ate it slowly, watching me. "What?"

"I didn't say anything."

"Exactly. You're just staring."

"I like to stare." I set the glass down and felt the drops of wine move over my tongue. With bold flavors that were innately fruity, it was a smooth vintage. But it was still no scotch. "I like to stare at my property."

"Really? So you just stand there and look at your truck?" she challenged, being a smartass.

I liked it when she was a smartass. "No. I like to stare at the beautiful things I own. You're the first piece of that collection."

Her fingers rested against the stem of her glass as her eyes softened slightly.

"Let's go home." I didn't want to sit through dinner and be tortured. Dinner was the prelude to sex, just boring foreplay. I was so hard in my jeans that my dick was about to pull down my zipper. Her pussy was already wet—that was a prediction I could make with absolute certainty. So let's skip the bullshit.

"We can after dinner."

"We can get it to go."

"Is sitting here with me that boring?" She sat perfectly straight, holding her gorgeous figure with pride. She had the sexiest shoulders, soft and rounded. Her hair was held back from her face loosely, and I wanted to yank the clip out of her hair so it would be free.

"Just the opposite."

"Then you can wait." She drank her wine again, smearing more lipstick against the glass.

I took an involuntary breath, aroused by her bossiness. As a hard man, I didn't respond to orders. I called the shots because I had to be in charge. If someone challenged me, I'd destroy them. But every time this woman put me in my place, it made me so fucking hard. She wasn't afraid of me like everyone else. If anything, she felt safe with me —invincible.

"Now have some bruschetta."

"No."

She rolled her eyes. "You told me you expect to die young. So maybe you should live a little while you can."

"I drink. That's how I live a little."

She ate another piece and didn't press me on it again. A crumb got stuck in the corner of her mouth, and her tongue swiped it away.

She was torturing me on purpose. "Your tongue is going to be raw when I'm finished skull-fucking you."

She hesitated before she took another sip. Her eyes

filled with playfulness, like she found that amusing. "When we're finished here, I'll get on my knees on the hardwood floor and push that dick as deep in my throat as possible. Spit will pool in the corners of my mouth, and tears will drip from the corners of my eyes because of your size..."

My breathing increased as the desire cut off my air supply. She was torturing me, but I couldn't stop picturing the scene she painted for me. Her strap would be pushed down, and her hair would be a mess from my fisting it so much.

"But for now, let's enjoy ourselves."

My nostrils flared.

She smiled. "I like torturing you. It's so easy."

"I can torture you too."

"But not as well as I can." She filled her glass with more wine.

This woman had no power, but she somehow put me in my place so easily. She had her hands on the wheel, and she was choosing the route.

I was just along for the ride.

The waiter emerged and brought our dishes.

Thank fucking god. Let's get this shit over with.

Cassini and I didn't have a lot of conversation to share, but since I was a man of few words, that was preferable. We could sit together in silence and be perfectly entertained. A few exchanges of expressions were all we needed.

She dug into her pasta. "This looks good."

I cut into my chicken and took a bite, unable to stop picturing her naked on her knees. I wanted to choke her with my dick, but I also wanted her legs wrapped around my waist while I sank deep inside her. I wanted to look into those pretty eyes as I felt her tighten around me in a climax.

Now that we had our entrees, I didn't have to wait long until this night was over.

My gaze moved out the window when I saw several black SUVs pull up at the exact same time. The windows were blacked out, and the passengers were impossible to see. I was always on alert for anything unusual, and this seemed out of place.

Groups of men spilled out of the cars, all dressed in black. They didn't carry weapons, but they were probably stashed under their clothes since they were about to hit a public place. It must be Lucian's men, and their objective was to get Cassini back unharmed.

Cassini kept eating, oblivious to all of this.

"Baby, listen to me." My eyes followed the men as they moved to the front door.

She sensed the seriousness of my tone and looked up, setting down her fork.

"Lucian's men are going to hit this room in about thirty seconds—"

"What?" she said, her voice rising.

"There's twelve of them, so no big deal—"

"No big deal?" she shrieked. She looked over her shoulder and spotted the armored vehicles outside. "Oh my god, what do we do?"

"It's going to be fine." I rose to my feet and grabbed her by the elbow. "You're going to leave out this back door and run." I pulled her to the back entrance, a door only used in case of an emergency.

"What about you?"

"Baby, I'll be fine," I said with a laugh.

"Why don't you come with me?"

"Because they'll chase us. And I'm not the kind of man that runs. Now, go." I pushed the door open, and the fire alarm immediately went off. "Now run, baby." I smacked her on the ass and pushed her through the door.

24

CASSINI

The gunshots sounded just when I made it to the corner. Like bombs were striking the surface of the earth, it was so loud, the sound in my ears seemed muffled. My heels made it impossible to run, and I yanked them off so I could keep going.

My heart was racing so fast.

I had no idea where I was headed. I had no idea if I was safer out here than I was with Balto.

I hoped Balto would be okay.

The gunshots didn't console me. I feared he was bleeding on the ground, dying alone.

It was too late to do anything, so I kept running. I headed in a straight line, running so fast my legs hurt. My chest tightened because I was breathing hard. I didn't know where I was going, but I kept running like my life depended on it.

A black SUV pulled out from the side street and blocked my path. It was tinted and armored just like the others. Men dressed in all black immediately hopped out to snatch me.

"Shit." I veered to the right and sprinted down the alleyway. I was a fast runner, but there was no way I could outrun five athletic men. Thankfully, they wouldn't shoot me, so I didn't have to worry about a bullet to my back.

I barely made it to the other side of the alleyway when one of the men charged into me and knocked me to the ground.

I hit the concrete hard, my body aching at the collision.

"Got her." The man grabbed me by the wrists and tried to cuff them together.

I kicked him hard in the gut.

His hand shot out and slapped me across the face. "Lucian said we could rough you up a bit."

I recognized his face and his voice. He was one of the men I saw at the estate on a daily basis. "Please let me go."

He got the cuffs over my wrists. "Not a chance."

I kicked him again even though the fight was over.

"Bitch." This time, he punched me in the face.

My head smacked into the concrete from the force. My eyes stopped working for a second as my body absorbed the pain. I was going back to Lucian, and there was nothing I could about it. I would be beaten, tortured, and raped. Balto wouldn't be able to save me a second time—if he survived. "Please let me go. Don't make me go back to him."

Another man grabbed me and tried to yank me to my feet. "Not a chance, sweetheart. He said we get a go with you as our reward for capturing you." He grabbed my dress and yanked it up to reveal my bare legs and my thong. He whistled. "I'm not passing that up."

Now I really started to panic.

Gunshots erupted in the alleyway, so loud because it happened right next to us. Two bodies dropped and thudded against the ground.

The men that handled me released me and turned around.

Another fell to the ground.

Now only two were left. They rose to their feet and reached for their guns.

A deep voice filled the alleyway, instilling more terror than those gunshots. "You want a go, huh? How about a go from me?" Balto emerged, his gun pointed at my first assailant. He looked uninjured. But he also looked pissed. He shot one in the arm then knocked the gun out of the other's hand.

I stayed on the ground, still frightened even though I'd been saved.

Balto gripped one by the neck and slammed his fist into his face over and over, making blood spray across the concrete next to me. He held the man suspended from the ground at the same time, hitting him until his body went completely weak. The screams stopped when his face was completely caved in. Balto dropped him to the ground.

I deliberately looked the other way so I wouldn't have to see it.

Balto moved to the other man, who lay injured on the ground. He dug into the man's pocket and fished out his phone. Then he made a call using the camera on the phone. "Lucian, I just thought you'd like to know that your men gave it everything that they had." Balto pointed the camera at the man as he placed his boot against his skull.

The man started to heave with terror. "But in the end, seventeen men still aren't enough for the Skull King." He slammed his foot down right into the man's head.

He screamed in terror.

Balto stomped his foot again. "I suggest you bring more men next time." With another stomp from Balto, the man's skull cracked and his screams were silenced. Death came for him, merciful. Balto pointed the camera back at himself. "Have a good evening, Lucian." He tossed the phone on the ground and stomped on it.

I lay there, my wrists still cuffed together. The threat was over, but I was still terrified, terrified that Lucian almost took me back. The men threatened to rape me, and they didn't hesitate before punching me in the face. Lucian was pissed, and he would be far crueler to me than he ever was before if he got me back.

I'd watched Balto shatter that man's skull, and now I couldn't unsee it. It was permanently ingrained in my mind.

Balto fished the key out of the man's pocket then kneeled down next to me. "Alright, baby?" He loosened the handcuffs then helped me sit up. His hand moved into my hair, and he examined the swelling in my face.

"I'm fine...you saved me."

"You really thought I'd let them take you?" The corner of his mouth rose in a smile, like this was all a game. "Not a chance, baby." His thumb swiped over my cheek as he felt the puffiness.

I gripped his wrists and closed my eyes, my heart beating so hard it actually hurt. Those few minutes were the most horrifying of my existence. The idea of returning to Lucian was far worse than the years I actually spent with him. I was so scared—and I wasn't afraid to admit it.

Balto held me that way for a long time, patiently waiting for me to calm down. "Baby, you're alright."

"I know…" I kept my eyes closed.

He gathered me in his arms then lifted me from the ground.

My arms hooked around his neck, and I buried my face in his shoulder.

Effortlessly, he carried me from that alleyway and back down the street where the restaurant was. As we approached the building, I heard the sounds of people gathered on the sidewalk, talking about the shooting that had just taken place. The police were there, but they didn't stop Balto. He put me in the truck then drove away, as if nothing happened, as if I hadn't almost been taken and raped by Lucian's soldiers.

Instead of staying in my seat by the window, I scooted to the middle and hooked my arm through his. My face moved to this shoulder, and I closed my eyes as I relaxed in his comforting presence. Somehow, he defeated seventeen men entirely on his own—and saved me from a fate I couldn't accept.

This man had been my captor for the last few months.

But now he was my savior.

25

BALTO

I carried Cassini out of the elevator and to my bedroom down the hallway. The incident tonight was normal to me, something I did on a nearly daily basis. There were always shootouts and battles that took place on the streets of Florence.

But she'd never seen anything like that.

I saw how scared she was as she lay on the ground with her wrists cuffed. I saw how she nearly burst into tears when the men threatened to rape her. And I saw the way she looked at me when I rescued her, the way her eyes filled with endless gratitude. She gave me a look I'd never seen before, like I was the only face she wanted to see.

Now she clung to me for comfort. She buried her face in my neck because being in my arms was the safest place in the world. Her fingers dug into me so deeply, it seemed like she never wanted to let me go.

I laid her on the bed, her strap falling down her shoulder just as I fantasized. She'd ditched her shoes during the getaway, so the bottoms of her feet were black and covered with dirt. Her eyes were still slightly wet from the terror, and the beautiful confidence she normally showed was long gone.

But I wanted her as much as I always did. In fact, I wanted her more.

I'd never been someone's savior before. I was always the nightmare, always the killer. But I liked saving her. I liked protecting her. And I liked how safe she felt with me. I sat at the edge of the bed and looked at her.

She sat up and unzipped the back of her dress so it would come free from her body.

The shootout didn't change my arousal. I wanted her badly before Lucian's men showed up, and I wanted her still. But she seemed too distressed for sex right now. I would normally dig my hands into her hair and take her, but I restrained myself.

She pulled the dress over her head and tossed it on the floor. The only thing underneath was her bare skin, her beautiful tits, and the little black thong she wore.

It was like she was trying to torture me.

She got under the covers. "Lie with me."

I stripped down to my boxers and left my gun on the nightstand. I got into bed, and the second my body was against the mattress, she cuddled into my side. She tucked her leg between my thighs, wrapped her arm around my waist, and laid her head on my chest.

My hand ran from the back of her neck down to her ass, gently massaging her as she sank into me. If she hadn't been there that night, I probably would have gone to a bar afterward and enjoyed a nice glass of scotch. Or I would have picked up a woman for the evening. I wouldn't have stopped living my life normally because of what I'd done.

But this woman had never seen a man's skull shatter like that. It was her first time.

"How did you kill all of them?" she whispered, her tits pressed against my torso.

I shrugged. "I just did."

"But there were twelve of them."

"That's not very many. Trust me." Lucian shouldn't have been so arrogant and should have sent more men. He'd thought he would catch me off guard at the restaurant, but the truth was, you could never really catch me off guard. I thrived during the unexpected. I adapted to new environments with alarming speed.

"And then you got to me so quickly."

"I run fast."

"They could have taken me back to Lucian... I was so scared. Being in his captivity wasn't so bad because I just accepted it. I behaved myself so things weren't so awful. But the idea of going back there...made me sick to my stomach. I panicked because I'd rather die than go back there. I also knew everything would be different. Lucian would hurt me so much now that he knows about our affair. My existence would be a million times worse than last time. If you'd arrived just a few minutes later—"

"I would have chased you down until I got you back. I've got allies everywhere. I would have stopped that car before it returned to Lucian's compound. And even if it did return, I still wouldn't have stopped. There's no scenario in which Lucian would have won."

She shifted her chin up so she could look me in the eye.

Her smoky eye makeup was smeared from the wetness in her eyes. Her seductive playfulness was long gone, but this uneasy version was just as sexy. "I was worried about you. When I heard the gunshots, I was afraid you didn't make it."

A smile melted across my lips. "It'd take a lot more than a few boys with guns to take me down. And you worry about me a lot."

"So?" she whispered. "Of course I do."

My smile disappeared. "That's cute, but you don't need to worry about me."

She shifted her body and moved onto my chest, her hair loose now that the pins had fallen out. Her lipstick had been wiped off on the wineglass, but her lips were still plump and kissable. "Thank you. I don't know what else to say." She rested on my chest like a cat, a small creature that felt weightless.

"You don't need to thank me, baby. You're my property —and I protect my property." I wouldn't allow Lucian to steal her away like that. If he wanted her, he would have to make an offer. I didn't just protect her to keep her safe. I did it for my own self-interest—because she was worth a lot. She might get me everything I wanted.

She tilted her head down and kissed my chest. Her full lips gently dragged against my hard skin. Her tongue poked out and tasted me as she moved, and her eyes closed at the same time. Her hands dragged across my chest and abs, feeling the grooves as she continued to kiss me. She migrated farther down, moving to my hard cock in my boxers.

My hard dick showed exactly what I wanted so there

was no denying my desires, but I didn't expect anything from her after what had just happened.

She hooked her fingers into my boxers. Slowly, she peeled them off so my cock could come free. Long, thick, and oozing at the tip, it was anxious to be inside her. Whenever I killed a man, I was particularly anxious to fuck a woman. It was an animal instinct, a carnal desire I couldn't explain. While I owned this woman and could do whatever I wanted, she clearly wasn't ready for that.

When my dick was free, she pressed her plump lips right against the shaft.

I closed my eyes and released a quiet moan. My hand automatically slipped into her hair because that simple kiss was enough to chase away all my coherent thoughts.

She dragged her tongue from the base of my shaft all the way to the tip. Then she kissed my crown, her warm breath splashing across my sensitive skin.

If I didn't stop this now, I would lose my strength. My hand tugged on her hair, and I kept her mouth away from my dick. "Baby, you don't owe me anything. At least not tonight." I lifted her chin so she could look at me straight on.

"I know I don't." She opened her mouth again, flattened her tongue, and then pushed me deep inside her.

My hand tightened in her hair, and I sucked in a breath between my teeth. "Fuck." Her mouth was almost as good as her pussy. It was definitely just as wet. I loved feeling her tongue gliding against my length, cushioning my cock as I drove deep to the back of her throat.

Her hand wrapped around my length, and she jerked me off while she deep-throated me. It was a great blow job, good enough to be paid for. She gave head like a hooker—a very expensive hooker.

All I'd wanted at the restaurant was this blow job, these plump lips surrounding my dick. But lying in bed with her, comforting her when she was scared, made me want something else. My arm circled her waist, and I rolled her to her back so I could move between her legs.

Surprise was in her eyes, but she didn't question my movements. Her legs immediately circled my waist, and her fingers dug into my hair. With enthusiasm in her eyes, she pulled me against her and pressed her sexy lips against mine.

I kissed her slowly, my lips touching hers sensually as I felt her petite body against mine. Her nipples were hard brushing over my chest, and her skin was so soft against mine. I breathed into her mouth and felt her breathe into mine as I pushed my crown through her tight entrance. Slowly, I sank, both of us breathing hard as we fell into each other.

My hand dug into her hair as I sank deeper, feeling every inch of that exquisite cunt. My fingers tightened in her hair and kept her in place as I entered the woman I kept on a short leash. Someone had tried to take her from me, but I defended her so easily. She would be mine until I decided to give her up—and not a moment sooner.

She moaned against my mouth then dragged her nails down my back. "Balto…" Her ankles unlocked, and she widened her legs so I could thrust deep inside her. Even if I tapped against her cervix and caused her pain, she didn't want me to stop. She wanted to feel every single inch of me no matter the cost.

My eyes locked on hers as I thrust into her, sinking us both into the mattress. "Baby, I'd never let anything happen to you." I would defend her with my life, torment Lucian every day by reminding him she belonged to me, not him.

With her legs wide apart and her tits shaking with the thrusts, she looked into my eyes with parted lips. "I know..."

26

BALTO

Cassini was quiet the next day, saying very little because she was still disturbed by the events of the previous evening. Her appetite was gone, and she spent most of her time looking out the window, like she might spot the armored cars coming down the street.

At the end of the day, I took her to bed, and she fell asleep shortly after sex. Her naked body was wrapped around mine, so I carefully pulled myself away without disturbing her. I got dressed then entered the living room just as the elevator beeped.

Heath stepped inside. "What the hell happened?" He helped himself to a glass of scotch then took a seat on the couch.

"Lucian is an idiot. That's what happened." I grabbed the decanter and helped myself.

Heath had let his beard grow over the last few days, so his chin was completely covered. He seemed too tired for basic hygiene. Now we actually looked different because I always shaved. I preferred a clean look because it showed off the hard bones in my jaw. "He must be watching you like a hawk, then. The one time you go out, he strikes."

"I don't care if he's watching me." He'd been studying me for months, and that was the best attack he could muster. What a waste of time. He had a perfect opportunity, but he blew it with his stupidity. "I don't understand how a man so brilliant can be so fucking stupid."

"Maybe he thought you would be unarmed." He swirled his glass as he looked into the contents.

"Which is even more stupid." I was never unarmed. The only time a gun wasn't within arm's reach was when I was buried deep inside a woman. If he wanted to kill me, that was the best time to do it.

"Arrogance is the number one cause of downfalls. Every regime in history has crumpled because of that reason."

"That may be the case. But Lucian doesn't have enough qualities to be arrogant. There's nothing to be arrogant about." The man knew how to connect wires to a motherboard and he knew how to outsmart Cassini, but he would never know how to outsmart me.

"So what are you going to do?"

"Nothing."

Heath raised an eyebrow. "Nothing?"

I nodded. "He'll come to me eventually. He'll realize the only way he'll get Cassini back is by giving me what I want."

"You really think he'll give up the diamond to get her back?"

He'd sacrificed seventeen of his best men by trying to catch me off guard. After realizing Cassini was cheating on him, he should have tossed her aside and forgotten about her. But now he needed revenge—against both of us. "Unless he sells the diamond, it's worthless. And if he tries to make a deal with someone, there's a good chance I'll hear about it. He's a petty man who can't stand hits to his pride, so he probably cares more about revenge than holding on to that diamond. Now he doesn't just want vengeance against me, but Cassini. The only way that's going to happen is if I give her to him."

"And how will he get vengeance against you?"

"By hurting Cassini. I'm sure once he gets her back, he'll plot something against me."

"So this is never going to end until one of you is dead." He pulled out a cigar from his pocket and lit it in my living room.

"Spoiler alert—it's not going to be me."

"So are you going to give her back, then?"

I stared into my glass, studying the sea of amber liquid. When I first started to drink, it burned my throat all the way down to my gut. Now it had no effect on me whatsoever. It was like drinking flavored water. "Not sure yet."

He puffed on his cigar and let the smoke rise from his mouth. "I assumed your answer would be no."

"Never assume anything when it comes to me." I was a man devoid of emotion. My decisions were always based on logic, nothing else. That was what made me a good leader. Even the hardest decisions were easy to make because there was nothing that complicated the matter.

"What do you even want the diamond for? You have the other two."

"Because all three belong to me."

"But you'll never sell them—"

"Because I don't need to sell them. Cassini will never be more valuable. It doesn't matter how beautiful she is. It doesn't matter if I respect her or like her. This is business, and unfortunately, she's the victim in that. But that's how the real world works."

He took another puff and let the smoke escape from the corner of his mouth. "I always knew you were cold, but damn…"

"It's my job to be pragmatic."

"But this has nothing to do with the Skull Kings. This is entirely personal—so you don't need to be pragmatic."

Maybe that was true, but it was still a betrayal to the man I was. I knew I would never have a serious woman in my life. It would be all work, drinking, and fucking. But then again, I'd never been with a single woman so long. I'd never been with a woman for more than a night. My regulars were all prostitutes, so they didn't count.

"Can you really do that to her?" Heath asked incredulously. "You've been living with her for months now. You're with her all the time. You killed seventeen men just to save her."

"I saved her because she's valuable property. It was nothing personal."

"Well, I don't believe that. I think you actually care about this girl, but you won't admit it to yourself."

"I never lie so that doesn't make any sense."

"People lie to themselves all the time. It's a defense mechanism. You can't stand the idea of caring about this woman, so you pretend she means nothing. You keep telling yourself she means nothing. You've said it enough times that you actually believe it."

I refilled my glass and brought it to my lips as I stared at the coffee table. "I can't have a woman in my life, at least not a permanent one. I'm the Skull King, and my obligation is to my men and our organization. There's no happily ever after with me. She would just be a liability, a distraction. There's no reason to keep her. I enjoy her now, but I can't enjoy her in the long term."

"Maybe that's true. But you would really do that to an innocent woman?" Heath was usually hard and cold like I was, but he obviously had a soft spot for Cassini. Maybe his tenure in prison changed his attitude about wrongful suffering.

"I don't care about innocent people. If I did, I wouldn't be the Skull King."

"You know what will happen to her." He stared at me as he held the cigar between his fingertips.

Lucian would beat her bloody. He would rape her, have his men rape her. He would torture her until he finally felt satisfied. Then he would kill her in a brutal way. It wouldn't be a bullet through the skull, something quick and relatively painless. It would be horrific, like drowning her in the pool or burning her alive.

"You're telling me you can just carry on like nothing happened? Knowing the woman who has been in your bed every night was now being tortured?"

"What other option do I have? I can't let him keep the diamond."

"It's just a diamond, Balto."

"One of the most expensive diamonds in the world."

"So?" he asked with a shrug. "You don't have enough money already?"

"He betrayed me, Heath." I slammed my glass on the table. "We had a deal, and he betrayed me. You think I can just let that go?"

"You got your revenge when you slept with his wife. If you ask me, that's worse."

"Not worse enough…" I stared at the coffee table.

"If Lucian does make the offer, really think it over. I know you'll regret handing her over."

"You don't know anything, Heath. I threw you in jail for six months, remember? Lucian's soldiers are just working for a paycheck, but that didn't stop me from crushing one's skull with my boot and recording it for Lucian to see. I'm a heartless son of a bitch."

"Well, I deserved to be thrown in jail. We both know it. And Lucian's soldier would have raped Cassini if he got his way. You don't need to feel bad for what you did. But Cassini is different. Let's not forget that you hunted down her ex-boyfriend and tortured him for what he did to her. She didn't ask you to do that. You weren't obligated to do it. But you did it anyway. What does that say about you?"

"She deserved vengeance. That's all."

"And you don't think she deserves to be free from Lucian?" he questioned. "Beating the shit out of Evan doesn't help her, Balto. It doesn't make a difference. It only satisfied your rage. You say it was for her, but we both know that's bullshit."

I rubbed my hands together as I stared at my hard knuckles. Maybe I did care about Cassini, but not enough to change my plans. When I took her, I'd always had the intention of selling her back. I just wanted leverage against Lucian so he would give me what I wanted. I was too stubborn to change my mind. "Let's drop it, alright?" I grabbed my glass again and finished the contents. "We've got work to do." I rose to my feet and grabbed the gun off the counter.

Heath put out his cigar even though he wasn't finished with it and came to my side. "Alright. I've said my piece."

We headed to the elevator so we could ride to the lobby. I hit the button then we waited for the carriage to rise all the way to our level. Heath pulled out his phone and checked his text messages before he shoved it back into his pocket.

"Balto?" Her quiet voice sounded from behind me.

I turned around to see Cassini standing there, swallowed by my enormous t-shirt. It reached all the way to her knees, and the sleeves touched her elbows.

Heath abruptly turned around and faced the elevator, knowing it would piss me off if he stared at her when she looked so sexy in my clothes. "Pretend I'm not here..."

Cassini stared at me with hurt in her eyes. "Are you leaving?"

I stepped toward her and heard the elevator doors open behind me. "Yes."

"And you weren't going to tell me?" She crossed her arms over her chest, her eyes bright with fire.

Heath stepped inside then hit the button. "I'll wait for you downstairs..." The doors shut.

I kept my eyes on her. "You were asleep."

"You could have woken me." She shifted her weight to one hip, her attitude vicious.

"I hoped I would be back before you even woke up."

"And what if I woke up and you weren't here?"

"You would have called me—that's what a phone is for." I didn't appreciate being questioned like this. I didn't appreciate her entitlement. I came and went as I pleased, and I didn't owe her anything.

"Don't be an asshole."

"Don't expect anything out of me."

The flames in her eyes continued to rise higher and higher. "Where are you going?"

"The same place I always go." Anytime I left in the middle of the night, I was heading to the Underground. It was my home away from home. It was where my men gathered and we plotted our next scheme.

"Don't you think it's a little soon for you to be leaving?"

"It's eleven. It's later than normal."

"I meant leaving me." She tightened her arms across her chest. "I'm not ready to be alone right now."

Her neediness aroused me, but it also pissed me off at the same time. "I have work to do, Cassini. I can't stay here with you."

"You're the Skull King. You can do whatever you want."

"And as the Skull King, I never abuse my power. I'm the leader of my men, and I've earned their respect and trust. I'm not going to turn my back on them just because you want me to protect you like a fucking guard dog."

The fire in her eyes died away, replaced by a painful expression.

"You're my prisoner, Cassini. Let's not forget that." I turned to the elevator and hit the button.

"Then why do you call me your woman?" she demanded. "Why do you call me baby?"

I stared at her, my expression stoic.

"You could have at least told me you were leaving."

"I don't owe you anything. Stop acting like I'm your boyfriend, and remember that I'm your captor. I'm your master. I come and go as I please. The only thing I'm required to do is make sure you have food and water."

That made her snap. She stormed toward me and smacked her hand across my face.

I allowed her to do it because I knew I deserved it.

"You're two different people." Her voice was surprisingly quiet for how tense the moment was. "When you're cold and ruthless, you're the Skull King. You treat me like a dog and make me feel insignificant. But when you're Balto, you're my protector, my lover, and my friend. You treat me with respect and make me feel safe. You call me baby as you make love to me. You promise that you'll protect me from all the terrible things in the world. You're always going back and forth, and I'm sick of it. Who are you? You can't be both. You can only be one or the other. So, which is it?"

I stared into her eyes, seeing the disappointment as well as the fury. I never realized the truth of her words until I was forced to confront them. I did have two identities. Before I met her, I was only the Skull King. I was only the killer, the conqueror, and the nightmare. But when it was just the two of us hidden away from the outside world, I was soft, kind, and gentle. I wrapped my arms around her and protected her. I turned into a man and forgot I was a monster. She softened me, made me weak. I didn't realize how far I'd fallen, how much this woman had changed me for the worse. Slowly, she'd corrupted me. Slowly, she'd turned me from a king into a man. I hunted down her ex and made him suffer because she had sunk her claws into me so deeply. She had a dangerous hold on me—and I had to shake it. "The Skull King. That's who I am."

27

BALTO

I sat on my throne and overlooked the men as they drank at their tables. I'd just finished a meeting with Brutus and Thomas, and we went over the taxes we'd collected for the month. Everyone paid in full—including the Cardello brothers.

But I hadn't really been paying attention because my thoughts were back at the compound, back to the moment when I walked away from Cassini. She made me realize how weak I'd become, how far I'd fallen. I was a strong man who refused to let anyone penetrate these walls, but she snuck by.

I shouldn't have let my guard down.

How could I have let this happen?

Heath sank into the chair beside me. "You look like a gargoyle."

My eyes shifted to his face, full of annoyance.

"You're hunched forward like you're about to jump on someone's head. Your eyes are all beady. Your jaw is clenched so tight—"

"I didn't ask you to elaborate."

"Whatever," Heath said. "I'm guessing the conversation didn't go well."

"No." I watched Denise move through the tables and serve the men their drinks. Her tits had two piercings through the nipples. The jewels sparkled in the dim light from the lamps that hung from the ceiling.

"It probably didn't go well because you were an ass."

"Irrelevant."

"What's the big deal? You have a beautiful woman who wants you home with her. God, I feel so bad for you." He rolled his eyes.

"She told me that I'm two different people. Sometimes, I'm the Skull King. And sometimes, I'm Balto, the gentle lover. I realized that I couldn't be both, that I never should have been both. So I left."

"What does that mean?"

"It doesn't mean anything. But when Lucian calls, I'm handing her over."

Heath gave me a disappointed look but didn't make an argument.

"Don't try to change my mind."

"I didn't say anything." He brought his glass to his lips and took a long drink. "Do whatever you want." He watched Denise move around to the different tables, her nipple piercings catching his eyes. "Why don't you call Lucian and make the offer, then? Speed up the process."

"That gives him all the power. He needs to come to me."

"Coming to him first does give you power. It makes it seem like Cassini doesn't mean anything to you. If that's the case, you really do have the upper hand. You took his wife, slept with her, and now that you're finished with her, you're ready to hand her back. You've made your mark."

That wasn't how I viewed her.

"No matter what you do, you have the upper hand. You know he wants her back if he sent those men to take her. You'll be in the position to make all the demands. You'll be able to get that diamond back along with his cooperation, easily. It's amazing that you met Cassini by mistake, just randomly in a bar. Because she solved all your problems."

When I spotted her in the bar, she stole my entire focus. With an elegant posture, beautiful eyes, and a tongue that could lick those olives so well, she was the kind of woman that gave me a hard-on the second I laid eyes on her. My only ambition at the time was getting a drink in my hand, but once I saw her, all I could think about was getting laid.

Then I fucked her—and wanted her again.

Our relationship wasn't just hot because she was sneaking around behind her husband's back. It was hot because she was such a good lover. She wanted me more than I wanted her. She made me feel like a god when I already knew I was a king. My dick stayed in my pants, and I became monogamous with a woman for the first time in my life—even though she was still sleeping with her husband.

But I wanted her so much that I didn't care.

Now we stood on the precipice of the end. I would hand her over—and she would have a violent death. "Yes...she solved all my problems."

It was five in the morning when I walked in the door.

Cassini wasn't on the couch like I expected her to be. She stayed in the bedroom, probably her own bedroom because we left things so poorly.

I stepped inside and flicked on the lights, realizing how alone I was.

I shouldn't have expected her to wait up for me, not after the way I'd treated her. Balto was dead, and the Skull King was there to stay. I never should have been so affectionate with her in the first place, not when it meant nothing. I gave her false hope about our relationship, made her expect things from me no one should ever expect. Getting rid of her was the best solution to my problem.

She'd been in my bed long enough anyway.

My phone vibrated in my pocket with a phone call. I pulled it out and checked the screen, surprised to see Lucian's name.

He read my mind.

This conversation was inevitable if he wanted Cassini back. I knew it was only a matter of time before he caved. He finally had the balls to contact me and concede the race.

I purposely let it ring a few times before I answered. I stood in front of the floor-to-ceiling window behind the dining table and looked out at the lights of the city. I knew exactly where his estate was located, so I stared in that direction as I took the call. "Couldn't sleep?" I loved toying with this man because it was so easy. Lucian possessed book smarts, being able to build weapons through math and science. But he lacked street smarts, something I excelled in.

"I never sleep."

"Because of the nightmares?" I teased. "That tends to happen after you see a skull get crushed like that. Sorry about your men, by the way. But you know how business goes..." I'm sure those men had families, people they left behind. And Lucian's paychecks probably never made the job worth it.

Lucian didn't respond to the taunts. "You have what I want. I have what you want. You wanna do this or not?"

"You're a terrible negotiator, you know that?" I slid my hand into the pocket of my jeans.

"I can't be that bad. I got your skull diamond, didn't I?"

The hair on my arms stood on end. "And I took your brother's life. Would you say that's a fair trade?"

Lucian turned silent.

"Not to mention, I've been fucking your wife around the clock—and she likes it."

He stayed quiet, but his rage was palpable over the phone.

Lucian was my most obnoxious enemy because he was untouchable. I had to keep him alive in order to find the diamond he took from me. If I barged into his compound and executed him, the diamond would be lost forever. It was the greatest life insurance policy he ever could have bought.

"Cassini for the diamond. We have a deal?"

"No. You know what else I want."

"And what would that be, exactly?"

"Play dumb with me all you want. I want your explosives."

"They're very expensive to make—"

"You want your wife or not?" I hated calling her that

because it didn't feel right. Even when she still lived with him and snuck off to my place, she never really felt like his wife. Just his prisoner.

"I'm willing to give you a specific number. But I'm not willing to commission the product indefinitely. Cassini isn't worth that much."

But she was worth a billion-euro diamond? "I want a hundred bombs."

"You're being greedy."

"You were greedy when you took that diamond without upholding your end of the bargain. This deal isn't just about the present. It's about the past. Give me a hundred bombs, or we don't have a deal."

Lucian sighed into the phone. "Fine. The skull diamond and a hundred bombs in exchange for Cassini."

I bartered until I got what I wanted, and now that it had happened, I didn't know what to do. I'd just agreed to hand over Cassini and never see her again. I should feel good about the deal, but instead, I felt my heart contract painfully. Was it guilt? Was it pain? I didn't know. "Why do you want her back so much?"

"Does it matter?"

"I'm curious." I stared across the city, seeing the lights illuminate this beautiful town. Lucian lived just on the outskirts, not more than thirty minutes away. Would I be able to look out this window again and not think of her? Would I be able to sleep in that bed and not feel guilty for what I did?

"She and I made a deal. She broke that deal, and now she'll pay for it."

"Like you've never had an affair."

"That's different. I own her—she doesn't own me."

"You're willing to give up so much just so you can hurt the girl?" I asked incredulously, finding that disgusting.

"Money is just money. I have plenty of it. But this is my wife. She humiliated me in front of the entire world. I will punish her accordingly. And then I'll pin her to the concrete next to the pool, and I'll stomp on her skull until it cracks."

28

CASSINI

I stared at his backside as I heard Lucian's voice in the silence.

I'll stomp on her skull until it cracks...

I covered my mouth to hide the gasp that wanted to emerge from my lips. My eyes watered with tears I refused to shed. I pictured myself on the terrace with the enormous pool, the place where I used to relax while he was at work. Now it would be the place where I would die, his boot slamming into my head until it finally gave in to the pressure and cracked.

Oh my god.

Balto hung up the phone.

I tiptoed back into my bedroom and got under the covers just in case he checked on me. It was impossible to keep my breathing calm and pretend to be asleep, so hopefully he would just ignore me and go to bed.

When I heard his heavy footfall enter his bedroom, I knew I'd been spared.

Now I could lie in bed and absorb the conversation I'd

just heard. After Balto and I became close, I assumed he wouldn't give me up to Lucian, but now I realized how wrong I'd been.

I never meant anything to him.

I'd always been a prisoner, even during the nights when I felt like something more.

He didn't say when he was going to make the trade, but I knew it would happen in the next few days.

What would I do?

Should I kill him in his sleep?

Should I try to run away?

Should I ask my brothers for help?

I had no idea what to do.

But I couldn't go back to Lucian. That wasn't an option.

Was I stupid for not being able to sleep when Balto wasn't here? Was I stupid for actually feeling safe with him? Was I stupid for not understanding just how vile he was?

Yes. I was so stupid.

***

It was easy to ignore him because he assumed I was angry about our recent fight.

He had no idea what the real reason was, so he never asked questions.

I went into the kitchen and grabbed something to eat before I walked back to my bedroom.

He sat at the dining table, eating his boring breakfast in his gym clothes. "Not talking to me, huh?"

I stopped and turned to him. "It's not like you want to talk to me either."

"I never said that."

"Not all things need to be said." I walked into my bedroom and ate lunch in the living room. I didn't have much of an appetite, but I forced myself to eat because these were the last few days of freedom that I had. I might as well eat something good while I could.

I looked out the window and tried to decide what to do first.

Should I call my brothers and tell them?

Say goodbye?

Or would that make them do something stupid and get themselves killed?

I didn't know how I could possibly get on the phone and tell them what was going to happen. That was a conversation I just couldn't bear. I'd cry so much that I wouldn't be able to get any words out.

I ate my donut and tried to enjoy it, but I barely could.

The door opened, and Balto walked inside, wearing a white t-shirt and sweatpants.

Would he tell me the decision he'd made? Or would he try to catch me off guard?

I didn't look up at him as I nibbled on my donut. "What?"

He approached the couch then stared down at me.

I looked up, hatred in my eyes. "What do you want? I'm not in the mood for sex right now. But I suppose you could just make me...that's something you would do." I shouldn't have expected Balto to do anything besides what he did—especially since he warned me about it. But I was disappointed in him. Was I stupid for thinking we actually had something? Maybe it wasn't love, but it was definitely *something.*

"When have I ever made you do something you didn't want to do?" He slipped his hands into his pockets and stared down at me.

He was about to make me do something I didn't want to do. "You're the Skull King, right? You're just a tyrant, not a man. That means you're capable of anything, including rape."

His eyes flashed with anger. "I deserve more credit than that."

"Do you?" I hissed.

His eyebrow rose.

"Get out of my room and leave me alone."

He continued to stand there. "I don't understand why you're so upset—"

"Because I thought I actually meant something to you." I tossed my plate with the donuts onto the coffee table. Invigorated because I had nothing to lose, I rose to my feet and stood up to this cruel man. "I didn't think you loved me, but I thought you cared about me. I thought we had something here. Maybe it was just passion and lust, but I thought it was something more. I thought we were friends. I thought we...felt things. When you rescued me, I never felt so safe in my whole life. I lost my parents, I was taken from my family because of a stupid decision I made, and then I came to you...and it felt like I belonged here. I've been a prisoner without any rights, but this place still feels like home. You don't fuck me like a whore. You move inside me with your lips locked to mine. You actually look at me. Ever since that night we met at the bar, it seemed like something was here. But now I realize...it was just me." I turned my gaze away because I could barely look at him. "I'm not a person to you. I'm just a product, something valuable that will come in handy eventually. I'm basically a pig being prepared for the slaughterhouse. The sex was just sex. The conversations were meaningless. All of this was meaningless."

29

BALTO

L ucian and I decided to make the exchange at his estate.

I'd drop her off, get my diamond, and the men would pile the explosives into the back of the van.

Straightforward.

I was bringing enough men to rival the military, so it would be stupid if he tried to screw me over again. If he did, I was prepared to kill him this time. Whether I got the skull diamond or not, I would be forced to put him in the ground.

Cassini and I didn't speak for the next few days.

She stayed in her room and ignored me as much as possible. She didn't want anything from me—not even sex.

It was like she hated me.

She would definitely hate me once she realized what was about to happen.

When it was time, I stepped into her bedroom and found her on the couch in her living room. "Come with me."

She slowly turned her head and looked at me, vibrant pain in her eyes. She didn't give me smartass back talk or tell me to leave her alone. The look she gave me was full of disappointment, like she despised me with every fiber of her being.

"Don't make me ask again."

She turned off the TV then rose to her feet, her eyes still lacking that innate light she always possessed. She approached me with her gaze averted, like looking directly at me was too much.

She didn't ask where we were going.

I didn't want to tell her anyway.

We stepped inside the elevator and hit the bottom floor. My men were already ready to go, so I climbed into the black SUV that she and I would share privately.

She got into the passenger seat, buckled her safety belt, and then looked out the window.

It was unlike her not to ask questions.

I pulled onto the road, and the men followed behind me.

With one hand on the wheel, I kept thinking about the deal that was about to go down. All I had to do was hand over this woman, and I would finally get what was mine. That skull diamond never should have been his in the first place. It was a mistake to sell it to him.

Just like Cassini shouldn't have been his in the first place.

We drove through the city in silence, and she still didn't say a word.

I used to be annoyed with her back talk, but now, her silence was much worse. She was indifferent to me, like I wasn't even in the car with her. I was just a ghost. "You don't want to know where we're going?" A part of me wanted her to fight me, wanted her to demand her freedom. It wouldn't change my mind, but at least she would be returning to Lucian with some fire under her tail.

"Yes." She kept her gaze out the window.

I turned to her, my heart slowing down. "You do?"

"You're taking me to Lucian."

My heart stopped beating altogether, just for a second in time.

"He'll torture me. Then he'll kill me by crushing my skull—just the way you do to your enemies." Her voice dripped with indifference, like her own death didn't scare her at all.

That night I came home, she must have eavesdropped. She must have been waiting for me, after all. "If you knew, why didn't you do something?"

"Like what?" she asked. "If I told my brothers, they would get involved and get themselves killed. If I slit your throat in the middle of the night, your men would turn on me, or Lucian would hunt me down. If I ran away, you would just find me again. Or Lucian would. Unfortunately, there's just no way out for me. There's never been a way out for me. There's no point in fighting it. You're doing exactly what you said you would do—and I'm an idiot for thinking you would change."

Her defeat hurt me, deep inside my chest. I'd never given up in my life, even when I was outnumbered and outresourced. But this woman had no chance. She'd never had a chance. Evan tricked her for a paycheck, and Lucian wanted to torture her. I used her to get what I wanted. This woman had been a slave for most of her adult life.

It was wrong.

She didn't look at me once. "Every time I think there's a glimmer of hope, I'm wrong. And those moments hurt far more than anything else. Hope is a dangerous thing. I would rather die and get it over with instead of wasting more time on hope."

I hated the tone in her voice. It didn't sound like her at all.

I kept driving, and I was approaching the edge of the city. Soon I would emerge into the countryside and approach his private estate. My foot stayed on the gas, but it itched for the brake.

I didn't owe this woman anything. She'd been a power move since the beginning. I only used her for vengeance and as a poker chip. But every fiber of my being didn't want to do this, even if this woman would never mean anything to me.

I pulled over to the curb.

She finally turned to meet my gaze, her eyebrows raised at the sudden stop.

I stared at the empty street ahead of me, knowing this was a bad choice. Keeping this woman would only hurt me in the end. I would never get back that skull diamond, and Lucian and I would be at war with each other until one of us killed the other. It was definitely the wrong decision to make.

But there was no other option.

I turned my head to meet her gaze, to see the emotion that immediately lit up her eyes. It was a beacon of hope, a desire for change. She looked at me the same way she did before, like I was her savior.

I liked it when she looked at me like that.

Her whisper filled the truck. "You aren't going to give me back to him..."

I held her gaze without blinking, hating myself for being so weak. This woman turned me into rusted iron. She took a simple problem and made it into a huge one. All she had to do was move those pretty lips and flash those green eyes and I was lost.

I wanted to be the Skull King.

But she made me into a man.

"No," I whispered. "I can't do it."

She threw off her safety belt then crawled into my lap. Her hands dug into my hair just the way they did when we were in bed together. Her plump lips pressed to mine, and she kissed me with the passion we always shared. As if nothing had happened in the past, we were lovers once more. Her fingers clawed at my body like she wanted to take me then and there, like she wanted me out of desire, not gratitude. "You promised me you would never let anyone take me..."

"Yes, I did."

"And you never lie." She rested her forehead against mine as she sat in my lap, her body tangled with mine.

"No...I don't." My hands moved underneath her shirt and felt the soft skin of her belly. Now I wanted to get her home and get her naked. It'd been days since she'd let me have her, days since I'd been buried inside my woman. I didn't just want sex. I wanted everything that we shared.

"Then what are we going to do? Lucian won't just let me go."

"No, he won't." He would come at me as hard as I would come at him.

"What does that mean?"

It meant only one thing. "I have to kill him before he kills me."

ALSO BY PENELOPE SKY

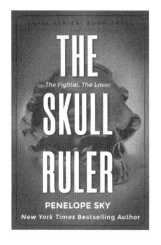

Instead of handing me back to Lucian so Balto can get everything he wants, he keeps me.

He pledges to fight for me until I'm free.

But as the weeks pass, freedom isn't as appealing as it used to be. This place has become my home.

This man is my home.

I'm not sure if I'd ever want to leave...even if Lucian was dead.

Order Now

WANT TO ORDER SIGNED PAPERBACKS?

Would you love a signed copy of your favorite book? Now you can purchase autographed copies and get them sent right to your door!

Get your copy here:

https://penelopesky.com/store

Due to the high volume of submissions, books are only shipped once per month. It may take 6 weeks to received your signed book. US orders only at this time